11/5/17

To Wendy & Mark.

Hope you enjoy your
new car as much as I did.
A lot of strange factors on
the way we met.

Herb.

Pooles Island

A Novel by

H. C. Creech

Mill Creek Press
Salt Lake City, Utah

Library of Congress Control Number: 2008937318

ISBN: 978-0-9798455-9-8

Printed in the United States of America on acid-free paper

pfb32975
First Edition

Cover by Tom Scheuerman

For My Wife Kerry

. . . for putting up with my constant sailing!

Preface

My wife Kerry and I are sailors and routinely sail past a small, but beautiful island on the Upper Chesapeake Bay. The island is Pooles Island, Maryland. Years ago, sailing past the island to one of our favorite destinations, Worton Creek, Maryland, I began to daydream. I had heard stories about the island, but really did not know anything about it other than the fact that the U.S. Government, specifically the Army, owned the island and that it was restricted. You can sail very close to the island, in fact, within about 30 yards of the southern tip, but landing is prohibited and dangerous. Pooles Island is part of Aberdeen Proving Ground and is within their firing range. Warning signs throughout the island warn of unexploded ordnance. I have no doubt that given the mentality of some of the local inhabitants of this region those warnings have been ignored and many beer parties have taken place on its shores.

As I mentioned, it is a quite beautiful island, and I would daydream and wonder about its actual history. Surely someone in the past had landed on and taken residence on this island? I started to research to find all I could about the island and discovered some fascinating details which are elaborated at the end of this book..

What I finally decide to write was a historical fiction novel about the inhabitants of this island, how they got there, and their adventures. The period I chose was the years leading to and including the beginning of the American Revolutionary War. The story takes place between 1746 and 1780 and follows the adventure of three young boys who come from very different backgrounds, Ezra, Zeeney, and Toby. You will come to understand that Toby and Zeeney are actually slaves and Ezra is their slave master, well not really but you will see. The three boys grow up and start their adventure at North Point

Plantation, although a fictional place, the land is the location of modern day Sparrows Point Steel Mill. If you have ever driven through Baltimore you would have surely noticed Sparrows Point and would find it hard to believe that such a place as North Point Plantation could have existed, but please keep in mind that this takes place over two hundred and fifty years ago, so it really is not all that farfetched.

Everything that happens at North Point Plantation and Pooles Island could have actually taken place. The boys build and learn to sail a small boat and go on the first of many adventures in their young lives. Sailing is a large part of the novel and therefore sailing terms are used throughout the book. But don't worry, if you're not into sailing, that's fine, this book is more of an adventure story than a textbook on sailing. Just in case you want to know the meaning of the terms, there is a glossary at the end of the book.

Thanks to Julie Chaplin, Tom Scheuerman, and Jackie Kahl for their help.

I hope you enjoy the story as much as I enjoyed writing it!

H. C. Creech
Baltimore, Maryland
September 1, 2008

North Point Plantation

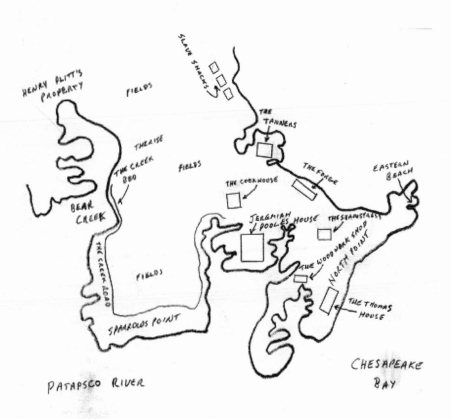

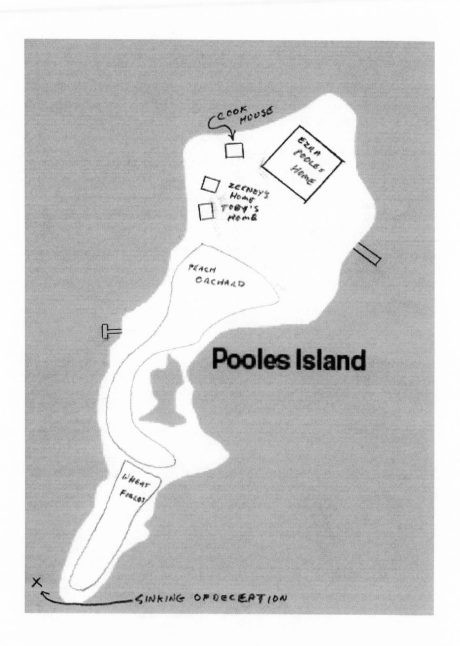

Pooles Island

September 1780

Chapter 1

Cyrus was anxious. He couldn't wait. The supply boat sailing from Baltimore was due at any time and he was eager for its arrival. Workers who lived at the plantation in Bowleys Quarters were anxious as well as the arrival meant that their long day was over and they would be transported back to their shacks at Bowleys. The peach orchards were teeming with fruit destined for Baltimore and Philadelphia, but tomorrow awaited and only so much fruit could be shipped in a given day to avoid spoilage.

Cyrus finally saw the tip of the mast rounding Miller's Island and knew that within two hours his chores would be completed for the day. With the prevailing southerly wind that was typical for this time of year, George Samptom was having an enjoyable and easy sail. This would be true of the relatively short trip to Bowleys Quarters but he did not relish the prospects of the beat back to the mouth of the Patapsco River. Once there his trip back to Baltimore would be relatively uneventful as long as the prevailing wind remained or if there was any wind at all. These uncertain conditions always affected George's workday, making it impossible to know what time he would arrive back in the Port of Baltimore. Uncertainty was the only certainty that existed in life of a sailing captain on the Chesapeake Bay.

As the boat finally pulled up to the dock on the lee of Pooles Island and George's crew luffed the sails to assure a slow arrival at the pier,

Cyrus threw lines to assist the boat's arrival. Once tied up, there was a flurry of activity as the workers hustled to load crates of unripened peaches onto the deck of the boat. This left just enough room for them to lie down and nap as the boat made its way back to Bowleys Quarters. As was typical, Cyrus and George had short, but pleasant, conversation. As time was of the essence, there was no room for idle chatter. Cyrus was anticipating his short walk back to the plantation on the northern side of Pooles Island. Totally unaware of the actions that would take place in mere hours. The Nanticoke scouting party observed his actions from the mainland just several thousand feet from the dock's location. As he shoved the boat from the dock and George tightened the main sheet, wind filled the sails and the Carol Ann slowly drifted away, gaining speed as it headed toward Bowleys Quarters.

Buckhorn was eighteen years of age and leading a raiding party for the first time. His braves were readying their canoes for the coming attack. Their plan was to kill the men and to return to the main body of their tribe with prizes from the island, the Nanticoke, that were camped on a small un-named island just east of the raiding party. As Buckhorn had never actually killed a man or woman in combat, he was unsure of how he would react. He was sure, however, that he would fulfill his duty because the results of his raid would guarantee the survival of the tribe as fall and winter approached. The plan was to attack, leaving no one alive, and transport anything that would support the tribe back across the small channel between Pooles Island and the mainland. As failure was not a consideration, rafts had been lashed together and waited along with the canoes to be used to transport any booty acquired in the upcoming raid.

Colonel Bowleys, a hero of the French and Indian War, sat on his porch swing as he as accustomed to doing at this time of day, leisurely watching the boat returning his workers from Pooles Island. This arrangement was working perfectly for the Colonel, as his plantation was no longer a producing farm, raising just enough to sustain his family and the workers that remained on the property. Colonel Bowleys had freed his slaves a year earlier; he now considered them to be workers, but he did not have enough work on his plantation to support them.

When Mr. Pooles had approached him regarding the arrangement, he thought it ideal, his former slaves would stay on his plantation working at Pooles Island during the day. Colonel Bowleys would receive a small portion of their pay for arranging the deal. They would be transported to Pooles Island each morning and returned back to their homes at Bowleys Quarters each evening. Colonel Bowleys had brought with him a primitive telescope that was a souvenir from the war. He used it on the porch to monitor the progress of the sailing vessel. Without the telescope he would not be able to see the actions of the boat with any clarity. With it, he could just barely make out the actions of the boat as it left the dock. Given the good prevailing wind he knew the small boat would easily make the trip from Pooles to his plantation in less than two hours. His daily ritual was to sit on the swing and doze, waking occasionally to check the progress of the transport boat.

Buckhorn readied his raiding party. The anticipation of the raid had his braves in a nervous sweat, even though the day was not as hot and humid as was normal for this time of year on the Chesapeake. As the Carol Ann was well out of sight Buckhorn motioned to his braves to launch their attack. As the only outcome to follow was victory, Buckhorn knew he had all of that evening and into the following morning to ferry the rafts to and from Pooles before the boat from Bowleys returned in the early morning to deliver the workers for the next day's work. Buckhorn had watched this recurring event as they planned their raid in the weeks prior to the full moon that would illuminate the sky the night of the raid. Their only concern was whether it would be a cloudless night. If not their trips to and from the mainland would be difficult, if not impossible. Buckhorn, although young, was very realistic but also very optimistic as he knew in his heart that the Great Father would not fail him and that a bright moon would guide his flotilla throughout the night.

Chapter 2

The Marquis de Lafayette, barely four years older than Buckhorn, but already a Major General in Washington's new army, was on the bow of a barge slowly making its way down the Chesapeake from the Susquehanna River. Having been in Pennsylvania fighting the British as one of Washington's generals, he looked forward to the break and the better accommodations that awaited him at Pooles Island. Previously, the British had occupied most of the Upper Chesapeake and had conducted raids throughout most of the tributaries to quash any resistance to their authority. Pooles Island had not encountered any interference by the British. The British felt that the Pooles were loyalists and that the remote and isolated location of the island made it strategically unnecessary to bother. Lafayette had corresponded with the Pooles family and made arrangements to have dinner at their plantation house that evening, as his troops would bivouac on the island for a week of rest and relaxation. He would camp on a down mattress rather than the hard ground beneath a tent. Lafayette was a man of great refinement and planned ahead on trips such as this to assure accommodations as those enjoyed by the Pooles. Although their peach plantation was in a remote location, they possessed luxurious refinements unknown to most in the colonies.

Cyrus' father was Ezra Pooles, he had come to Maryland from England as a small boy. His father was a merchant who had export connections with England and had established a prosperous business located on his plantation in North Point, just east of the growing Port of Baltimore. Ezra, living a life of privilege, and with an abundance of idle time, loved to explore his new home. He had two slaves approximately his age assigned as companions to explore with him. Toby and Zeeney were more like brothers than servants to Ezra and he treated them accordingly. All three shared in planning most of their adventures. Ezra did not consider himself their master, but rather thought of them as co-conspirators in adventure. Ezra's parents did not approve of his disappearances for days at a time while he explored and mapped his new and undiscovered water paradise. By the time Ezra was caught, he always had an excuse and he knew that his father's busy schedule would work to his benefit.

Ezra was twelve years old; he was born on July 8, 1733. He was tall and lanky for his age. At nearly five feet six inches, he was taller than most of his friends. This was especially true of Toby and Zeeney, both of whom were about four inches shorter than Ezra. Ezra was fair complexioned, like his mother, and had dark, almost black hair similar to what his father told him he had had when young. His striking green eyes gave him, at his young age, an almost handsome appearance.

Toby and Zeeney were brought to this land as babies and did not really remember anything about their former land. They knew they were of the same tribe, but did not think they were related. Neither knew their birthdays, but assumed they were about the same age as Ezra, even though he was so much taller. Since they did not have birthdays, they asked Ezra if they could share his. No problem was his response; it would mean that they would just have a bigger party.

Toby had dark hair and was equally dark in complexion, while Zeeney was lighter skinned and had a reddish tint to his hair. The only things they had in common, beside their race, was their height and similar colored chestnut brown eyes. Of the three boys, Zeeney was, without doubt, the quickest of mind. He would grasp things quickly and had no problem with even the most complicated situations. Toby, on the other hand, was not as quick to learn new things and generally let Zeeney take the lead in any new situation. Ezra, while not quite as bad as Toby, was slow at learning, new things, but he seemed to excel in these things once he had mastered them.

The three "brothers" decided to fashion a sailing canoe that Toby and Zeeney's people had described from their remembrance of the old land, the land from which they had been stolen and transported to this new and alien environment. The only common denominator was that of water. The tribe from which Toby and Zeeney's family was taken lived on the shores of the Ogooue River. The river was so much a part of their livelihood that they were attached to it and learned to navigate it for most of their food. Canoes were built and later sails were added to aid the tribe in getting to the better fishing grounds. Although Toby and Zeeney were too young when captured and brought to the New World, their family told many stories about the former life and drew pictures in the dirt of the sailing canoes that sustained the tribe.

Zeeney loved to play mind games with Ezra, even though he was a slave. He knew he was brighter than Ezra. As far as Zeeney was concerned, Ezra was his brother and equal; he did not understand any system other than the elementary existence that ruled his life.

Ezra initially went along with the other two boys, but he confided to them that he had a problem with any type of boat. Ezra's oldest brother Zachary, had died when Ezra was one year old. Ezra did not remember his brother, but had been constantly reminded as he grew up that Zachary had attempted to take a boat he and friends had built on the Chesapeake. On their first attempt to sail the boat a sudden storm came up, swamping the small boat and drowning Zachary and his two best friends. Ezra mother and father reminded their children how dangerous the bay was and forbade them to ever venture beyond the shallow surf at Eastern Beach, where the family summered each year.

Ezra told Toby and Zeeney that there was no way he could build a boat, if his father and mother found out he would be in deep trouble.

Zeeney pleaded with Ezra, "Without a boat we can't get off land and with all of the water that surrounds us we won't see anything."

Ezra finally agreed, but told the other two boys that the only way they could do it was in complete secrecy. So it was agreed, they would build a boat. What type or size had not been established, but they would use every means available to hide the existence of the boat from friends, and especially family.

Once the tree was found that would be the source for the boat, the fun began. They chose a large loblolly pine tree not far from the property on which they lived. Not knowing loblolly pine from elm, the three boys decided that pine was good because the needles floated better in Bear Creek than leaves from other trees. Also, the pines seemed straighter, and the branches were higher up the tree than other trees in the area. Bear Creek was many minutes from the North Point plantation and Ezra, Toby, and Zeeney fished there on a regular basis.

The creek formed a passage west from the North Point plantation to the Patapsco River. Once the loblolly pine tree was chosen, their next problem was how to fell the tree. Toby, Zeeney, and Ezra, being only about twelve years old, did not really understand how to bring down a tree. They could conceptualize the final design of the sailing canoe they wanted to create, but bringing down the tree was not completely established in their collective minds. Zeeney decided that he was the real creative genius of the group and would come up with a solution. He knew that his family used plow horses to remove stumps from the fields and felt that this was the direction to go. Unfortunately for Zeeney, he did not understand the difference between a two thousand pound stump and a thirty-ton tree. Toby knew they would have to find some other way to cut the tree down as well as implements to hollow out the canoe once it was on the ground. Ezra had been with his father when the slaves were clearing fields and knew there was a saw and other tools on the property. He just had to figure out where they were and a way to "borrow" them to complete their mission. He remembered a shed near Bear Creek that most likely held the tools. It was probably locked, but that would not deter Ezra and his band of adventurers. They planned to go to the shed the next day and begin their ultimate adventure.

Early the next morning they packed a food bag to sustain them for most of the day. The boys discussed their project and determined that it would take weeks to complete, maybe even more given the unavoidable chores they were assigned. Ezra would have to devise a plan that could free them up to work on their sailing vessel. He was the only one that could make reliable alibis for the three of them. This would take some planning. He remembered that his father, Jeremiah, wanted an area cleared near Bear Creek, but did not want to assign these tasks to his men because it was planting season and that could

not be delayed. His father was very busy this time of year and would probably not even check on the boys and their progress. They could work on the project for weeks, uninterrupted, and worry about the punishment for not completing the assigned task later.

Perfect!

They would put aside about a hour each day to work on the clearing. This way, if they were caught, they could plead that they were just slow workers. Even more perfect!

They were off. Once Ezra had convinced his father that they were about to do a legitimate chore, they would not even have to break into the shed to steal the tools. Ezra's felt brilliant.

Ezra approached his father in the field.

"Father," he said, "may I take Toby and Zeeney down to the creek bed that you wanted cleared? We're really bored."

Mr. Pooles could not believe what he was hearing. Ezra had never volunteered for anything, especially a project that Mr. Pooles had wanted completed, but could not free up workers to finish.

He beamed, and as he did said, "Son, that is a wonderful idea, but you will need tools. There are all you need in a shed near Bear Creek. My key for that shed is in my office. Fetch the key, but don't lose it."

In the shed were all the implements they would need. A large two-man saw, in fact, two of them, hammers, chisels, boring implements, and other tools that would help them with their project, but first they needed the saw. They had already decided which tree to cut down. It was the right type, a loblolly pine. It was straight and thick enough for them to carve the final design. The only problem was that the design was in their collective heads. They needed an actual written design from which to work. Toby found scrap parchment and lumps of coal in the shed. He decided that he could draw a rough idea of the plan and then modify it based on their discussions, but first things first, they had to cut down the tree.

Unfortunately, the three boys had never attempted a project as difficult and as potentially dangerous as this appeared to be. They were young and impulsive, but not stupid. They knew they needed a plan, one of safety as well as one that would position the tree in the proper place to finish their design. Zeeney remembered watching his family clearing the land and recalled that in addition to cutting large trees, with saws, they also used hammers and wedges. These he found in the shed. He discussed his thoughts with the other two boys and they agreed on a plan. The tree they had chosen was approximately 200 yards from the creek on a slight incline. This would be perfect as they would start cutting from the opposite side, away from the creek. Then as the tree started to lean, they would finish it off with the wedges and hammers. The result, they thought, would be that the tree would not only fall safely, but that, because of the incline, it would slide toward the creek.

They were wrong on both accounts. The large saw made easy work of the massive tree. Even though the boys were young, they were strong for their age and quickly cut through the tree by taking turns sawing. About two-thirds through the cutting they heard a cracking sound that indicated that the large pine was about to give up. It was time for the wedges and hammers. This took far longer and was much harder than they had anticipated. They carefully placed the wedges and started to hammer, but it was already obvious that the great tree was not going to give up that easily. They were now really concerned with safety issues. If one of them was hurt, even slightly, it would let Mr. Pooles in on their secret which he would quickly discover had nothing to do with the chores he had been sold on. Therefore, they decided they needed to take a different approach. They discussed their situation briefly and decided now was the time to abandon this stage of the process and devote the next hour to the fake clearing. They would start the clearing, work for about an hour, and then head home. They proceeded to clear, but with little enthusiasm.

The next morning arrived and the three co-conspirators headed out to finish what they had started the previous day. When they approached the area, they noticed immediately that the skyline had changed. There was a noticeable space not present the previous day. The boys were quite surprised when they arrived at the project site that the cutting they did the previous day had actually worked. The sheer weight of the tree and possibly the winds the night before had finished the job for them. Not only had the tree fallen in the wrong direction, but in falling it had kicked back severely to one side. This action would have clearly injured or killed at least one of the boys. They sighed a collective sigh of relief. None of them wanted to think about who might have been injured or killed. All they knew was that they had been terribly lucky. Now they had a new problem. Because the tree had fallen ninety degrees away from the direction in which they had intended, it was now resting in a hilly area that would make their work more difficult. They had no idea how to move the massive tree to the originally planned location. They would work on it in place then figure some way to move it later. Zeeney suggested that the time to draw up their plans was now.

They all knew that they would need a long enough vessel to accommodate the three of them as well as supplies to last several days. They did not plan any cabin area or shelter as they thought their trips would be short and that they could sleep ashore at night. They felt that the final design called for a boat at least 21' long and 4' wide. The tree would easily allow for the length, but not the width. Zeeney vaguely remembered sticks that extended from either side of the sailing canoes. These devices, the dirt drawings revealed, would stabilize the narrow boat, so they decided to incorporate some into their plan. They also planned on two sails, one forward and one aft. They knew they would have to fashion a rudder, but it was agreed that this final stage could be dealt with later, as well as the composition and source of the sails their yet to be named vessel would need.

The plans were roughly sketched on the parchment with the lumps of coal that Toby had found in the shed. They found a tree limb that was roughly the finished length of their planned vessel and cut another one for the width of the boat. They decided that these two limbs would be their "master guides" as they possessed no other measuring tools. They would protect these in the shed at night to assure that they would be used throughout the project. Other required measuring devices would be added, but these two would be marked and kept in safe keeping for the duration. The next step was to choose the appropriate section of the tree to cut the basic design, not too close to the trunk, but also not into the area where limbs started. After determining that this was not possible they decided to start the bow end slightly into the area where limbs formed because it was more tapered leaving the wide stern at about three feet from the base of the tree. Initially, they were going to do the first cut at the exact length of the master limb, 22', but then decided to go with a slightly longer 24' to leave room for error. They fashioned a new master-measuring limb but preserved the old, as that was truly the desired length. Next, it was time to cut.

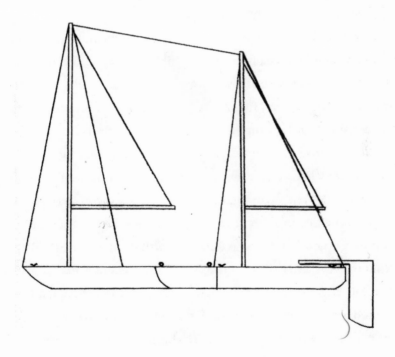

The large toothed saw made short work of the big tree and before long the boys had the rough finished length of their new boat. They then attacked the core of the boat with pick axes to hollow out the interior. They took great caution not to remove too much material knowing that the finish work would be tedious. Their work was becoming a labor of love and they were anxious to actually launch and sail their new vessel.

Several problems remained, however. None of the boys had ever sailed and Toby and Zeeney had never swam. Those concerns could be dealt with later. Their immediate goal was to launch. They couldn't wait!

Once the rough hollowing was done it was time to painstakingly chisel the interior to the finished size. They made sure that the two areas where the masts would go were actually thicker. They would finish those areas later once they had chosen and fashioned the masts. Things were going well and they were way ahead of schedule until it dawned on them that they had not really come up with a schedule . All they knew was that they wanted to finally see their boat afloat.

On the fourth day, they finally had the interior completed. They had even found time for the allotted one hour a day to clear the creek bed. This totally surprised the boys. They never thought they would be so disciplined. They had actually cleared enough land to cover themselves should Mr. Pooles check on their progress. They were not concerned about this because spring was the busiest time of year and had him totally preoccupied. They would continue with the charade just in case.

Now that the interior was completely roughed out it was time to think about the masts. Oak was chosen because of its strength, but the boys found it hard to fashion a proper finish because of the simple tools they possessed. They wanted the masts and booms to be as smooth as possible. Ezra discussed this with Toby and Zeeney. There was a woodworking shop on the property that used lathes to fashion poles for chairs and beds. This would be perfect to finish their masts and booms. They could fashion the items to rough sizes and lengths, but would have to come up with some convincing story to get the poles into the woodwork shop, completed, and get them back to the boat without creating any suspicion. Mr. Thomas ran the woodworking shop. He was certainly nice enough, but was totally devoted to Mr. Pooles. But Ezra had a thought. Mr. Thomas' pretty granddaughter, Elizabeth, was always flirting with Ezra. Maybe he could use her to get the masts and booms through the shop without any contact with Mr. Thomas. He would have to find a way to convince Elizabeth that they were being used for anything but a boat. He would also have to disregard his dislike of girls in order to complete his mission. All he had to do was come up with a convincing lie. Ezra's mother was having her birthday in three months. he would have to figure why she needed four long oak poles, one 18', one 16', one 7', and one 5'6", without raising suspicion.

"Well," he thought, girls are stupid anyway. I'll just make up a ridiculous story that she will believe."

The surprise aspect should work, but sooner or later someone would question why they never saw the unusual poles in the possession of Mrs. Pooles. Ezra decided that this risk was worth taking because by the time these questions would arise, the launch of the boat would be complete. The only remaining problem was devising the best and most believable lie?

Spring 1746

Chapter 3

Ezra saw Elizabeth down by the Eastern Beach, very close to the garden. She had apparently been picking vegetables for that evening's supper. Ezra approached her. He was about two years older and a good foot taller than Elizabeth, and she was in love. As Ezra got close she began to blush.

"Now or never," he thought.

"Elizabeth, did you know that my mother's birthday is this summer?" She said, She did not."

"Well, I want to surprise her, but I need your help. You know how mother loves to spend days on the beach in the summer and with her fair skin has trouble with the strong summer sun."

"Yes," Elizabeth said.

"Well, I have a plan and I need your help."

"What is it?" Elizabeth gushed, "I'd love to help."

"Here is my plan. I want to construct a very special tent for her to use on the beach, one that has many levels to circulate the heat. I have cut some poles to length, but they are too heavy to carry to and from the beach. If you could arrange for your grandfather to work them on his lathes, they would be perfect for the tent. But, it would have to be a surprise. We have to come up with a reason for you to tell your grandfather so he won't tell my father. Otherwise my mother will find out and the surprise will be ruined."

Elizabeth contemplated the problem and a broad smile crossed her face.

"Grandfather would do anything for me. I'll tell him they are a surprise birthday present, the truth also works best. Then he'll do it in secrecy and you can surprise your mother."

"Good then, I'll have Toby and Zeeney deliver the poles to your grandfather tomorrow. They are already cut to length, the boys will bring a drawing on how to smooth and taper them."

Ezra thanked Elizabeth for her help, excused himself, and then broke into a run to find Toby and Zeeney. He could not wait to tell them the news.

The next day it was back to the boat. Things were going very well. So well, in fact, that they devoted even more time than they had planned to clear the creek bed. Their next plan was to have the boat prepared and ready to accept the masts and booms that were being finished at the woodworking shop. Toby had already found long leather straps at the tanners. These were destined to be used as reigns for the horse wagons, and they were just long enough and thick enough to be used for two functions; one, to attach the booms to the mast, and two, to use for the mast rigging. Toby was a regular visitor to the Tanner's workshop. He knew that if he removed two or three straps at a time they would never be missed. As he had a couple of weeks before they would be needed he had plenty of time to get all the straps they would need. As he removed the straps he would hide them in his clothes and store them at the shed at the creek bed until they were needed to rig the boat.

Ezra woke the next morning with a start. It occurred to him that his brilliant plan to get Elizabeth's grandfather to lathe the poles was only half the problem. He also needed sails. He knew that he would have to appeal to Elizabeth's affections once more, and he wasn't at all happy about the prospects. The seamstresses worked in a building not far from the tanners. Ezra would need two sails, one 12'3" tall by 9' at the tack, and one 10' by 5'6". They had to be as light as possible but also impervious to the wind. They had to be fashioned in such a way that they could be easily rigged to the boat, but they could not look like sails. Ezra thought that this might actually be easy.

Elizabeth had already conspired with Ezra in the lie about his mother's birthday. He was also convinced that she believed his story regarding a tent. A tent isn't a tent without the top. He would just tell her he forgot to order the top! He just had to figure a way to make it look like a tent top, but still usable as sails on the yet to be named vessel. Ezra went back to the shed and retrieved the parchment and lumps of coal. He found a straight stick that he guessed was about a foot long. On this he made a mark with his knife at the midway point. He divided the two halves into halves, the remaining halves he divided again. This gave him a rudimentary measuring device to use to plan his tent top. The usable sails had to be cut out of the tent top without affecting the integrity of the individual sails, but they still had to resemble a tent top. After many trials Ezra came up with a plan. The two halves would be joined at their greatest lengths connected by a strip of thin material at their confluence. This strip could be easily cut to separate the two sails. On either sides of the strip would be reinforced pouches that would be slid down the masts. The sacrificial strip of cloth would not be pretty but would not affect the integrity of the sail where it joined the mast. Leather strap loops would be placed through the reinforced seam that matched the length of the booms and mast. At the apogee of each triangle would be extra reinforcement, ostensibly to be used to attach tent poles but in actuality the location of the greatest stress on the sails. A plan, however, had to be devised on how to raise and lower the sails. The final design was a large symmetric rectangle that incorporated both sails. Besides the sacrificial strip running down the middle there was waste material on either side of the two sails. All together it was one large rectangle.

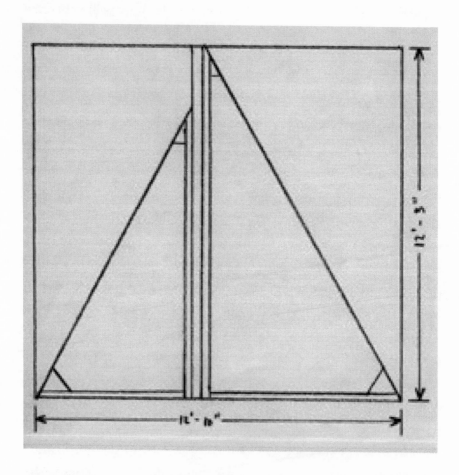

If Ezra conveyed his instructions correctly to Elizabeth and she, in turn, told the seamstress how important the details were, Ezra would have two usable sails with some waste left over. He had already decided that the two remaining triangles that were not sails could be used to fashion a rough tent for nights ashore once they left for their adventure.

One of Ezra's daily chores was to fetch water from the well. He knew that the well had a long length of rope and a simple block to assist in the raising of the heavy bucket. It could easily disappear, but he would need two. There were wells throughout the property, but he decided that if he were to remove the one near his house, it might draw too much attention. On the large property to the west, near Baltimore town, there were many wells, he could easily remove blocks from them without any notice. The next morning, instead of heading to the creek bed, the boys ventured onto the next property. They did this very early in the morning before the owners and workers of the property had started their day. The first well was easy pickings and had the bonus of being very deep, therefore it had an extraordinarily long rope that would come to be very handy. In fact, it was so long that at the next well they would need only the block. They decided to hide the rope and block in nearby brush as carrying it with them might raise suspicion, should they be discovered. After finding an appropriate hiding place, they proceeded to their next supply depot, the next well on the property.

Ezra boosted Toby up to retrieve the block, he just about had it removed when he slipped and fell head first into the well. Toby was very fortunate that it was a particularly rainy spring and that the water table was very high, additionally the fact that the bucket had been removed softened his splash into the well water. The fact that he did not know how to swim struck him as he plunged deep below the surface. At first Ezra's reaction was to go in after Toby, but he quickly realized that Zeeney was not strong enough to raise Toby by himself, let alone the larger Ezra. He yelled down to Toby, who was quickly panicking not to do just that. He would think of something. While he was thinking and Toby splashed in the depths below, Zeeney raced over to the bucket and slowly dropped it into the hole. They heard a loud thump followed by an "Ow," as the bucket hit Toby's head. Both

Zeeney and Ezra yelled down to Toby to grab the bucket. He did this gladly, sore head and all. It was very difficult for the two boys to retrieve Toby. As they would get him a few feet from the surface the rope would slip, plunging Toby back into the cold dark water. He had overcome his initial fear, but now the fear of an unknown creature that he was sure dwelled in the darkness of the well water nearly put him into a panic. He started to scream for Ezra and Zeeney to get him out. Zeeney looked around and saw a medium size tree about twenty feet from the well and had an idea.

"Don't panic!" He yelled down to Toby, Hold on! Ezra will hold you, and I'll be right back."

Toby, panicking even more screamed to Zeeney.

"Zeeney, please don't leave me. I'll die down here!"

Zeeney yelled back, " Don't worry. I'm going for help."

With that Zeeney took off. He raced back to the location where they had hid the long rope earlier that day. Zeeney knew that the rope at the well in which Toby had fallen was not long enough to reach the tree twenty feet away. His plan was to attach this rope to the other rope and use the tree as a form of a block and tackle in order to pull Toby from the well. As he knew Toby was in a state of panic, he ran faster than he had ever run before. He retrieved the rope and quickly returned to the well. Ezra was still doing his best to raise Toby, but the only thing he was capable of was holding him at the surface.

Toby knew full well that the monsters that resided in all wells would strike at any moment.

When Zeeney returned, he quickly attached the bitter end of the rope to the one attached to the bucket. He raced around the medium tree and then around two smaller trees nearby.

"Try pulling harder," he yelled to Ezra, and Ezra did.

As Toby slowly rose from the surface, Zeeney tied the rope to the last small tree, He pulled the slack in the line at the medium tree then the next small tree, and finally at the anchor tree which he retied. Toby, now inches out of the water, hung to the rope for dear life. He sat on the bucket and wrapped his legs around the rim. This gave him great relief. He was not yet out of harm's way, but he was no longer in danger of being devoured by the monster in the well.

Zeeney yelled back to Ezra to pull hard again, which he did. After each tug by Ezra, Zeeney would repeat the process of pulling the slack from the line and retie the anchor. It was working. Toby was slowly, painstakingly, being retrieved from what would have surely been his watery grave. Just as he reached the top and the exhausted boys gathered at the edge they heard a voice

"Can I help you boys?"

Chapter 4

Henry Plitt was out for his morning hunt. As the second-generation owner of the property that adjoined the Pooles' property, Henry knew every square inch. Each morning he would hunt for quail and ducks near the marsh that ran along the tobacco fields. He heard the commotion long before he arrived at the well that was used by the field workers during the hot, humid Chesapeake summers and fall. When he came over the rise that hid the well, he readied his musket and side firearm. It was not unusual to come across Indian raiding parties that were usually frightened off by the sight of a heavily armed white man. When he saw the exhausted boys, he was both relieved and confused. Who were they and what were they doing on his property?

His confusion continued as he noticed that besides being exhausted, one boy was soaking wet and there was a long length of rope wrapped around several trees. Henry put his weapon to his side and just stood there. He didn't say another word, allowing the boys to tell him why they were on his property, and why they were in the state they were in.

Ezra spoke first. "Sir, we were trying to fetch some water and Toby here fell in."

Henry replied, " Where did you come up with the extra length of rope?"

Zeeney offered the explanation, "When Toby fell in I remembered that we had passed another well and knew we would need more rope to pull Toby out. Ezra held him out of the water while I ran to fetch the rope."

Henry, looking quite skeptical, did not know quite what to say at this point. After a moment he said, "Alright, but as soon as you feel up to it, replace that rope on the other well before you leave my property."

The boys were crushed. Not only had Toby nearly drowned, but the whole purpose of their expedition was now an obvious failure. They were sure that they would not leave Mr. Plitt's property with the implements they needed and would have to devise another plan.

Their walk back to their plantation was the least enjoyable one that they had during their entire adventure. All three boys were terribly exhausted and Toby was particularly miserable. At least it was a fairly warm day so he was not really cold, but nonetheless, miserable. They had to devise another less dangerous plan. It was also obvious, at least to Ezra, that before they left on their sailing expedition Toby and Zeeney would have to learn how to swim. He could not be concerned about that on the trip. The boys did not say very much on their way back. They knew they were finished for that day and would return home without even bothering to stop at the creek bed. None were in the mood for working on a boat and Toby could not wait to change into dry clothes.

Chapter 5

The next day Ezra woke up feeling a little discouraged. Where was he going to find not one, but two blocks, and a long length of rope? His original plan would no longer work because he had no idea how far away other wells were. There just had to be another easier source. He got out of bed, washed his face, dressed, and walked over to the cookhouse to see what was cooking for breakfast. When he walked into the cookhouse, the first thing that he saw was the very block he needed, suspended above the fireplace holding a large cook pot in place. Ezra immediately walked over to the fireplace, almost forgetting his hunger. Anna May was a wonderful cook and treated all the boys, black or white, as if she was their mother. All the boys loved Anna May, especially for her cooking. Ezra then noticed not one, but three different blocks used to raise and lower oversized cook pots. He looked at their arrangement and even the way that the ropes ran over to individual iron cleats located on the wall that surrounded the large fireplace. These cleats were used to hold the cook pots at the desired height above the flames, and to raise them completely away from the fire to serve the hot stews or soups that Anna May was so skillful in creating.

Ezra, still admiring the blocks, said to Anna May, "Where do you get these?"

Anna May replied, "Old Mr. Jim over at da workshop makes dem for de plantation, he made dem many years ago and dey works just fine. Why you ask?"

Ezra replied, "Oh, no reason, just curious."

Well, Anna May said, " you take your curiosity and dis stew over to dat table and eat. I got hungry peoples to feed."

Ezra did take the stew to the table, but as he ate he stared at the blocks and cleats and knew where he was headed after breakfast. He would go to see Old Mr. Jim and his workshop. He ate as fast as possible. He could have eaten more, as the stew was particularly good that morning but his desire to obtain the blocks was more overwhelming. He headed straight for Old Mr. Jim's workshop not really knowing what he would do once he was there. He thought that at the very least he would find out what was available and how Toby would be able to procure them. The workshop was a fair distance from the cookhouse and now Ezra was regretting that he did not eat more stew, but dinner was not all that far away and he just could not wait any longer. Once at Old Mr. Jim's he noticed an enormous amount of activity. He guessed this was because it was planting season and the plantation would need a lot of replacement items in the coming year. The workshop consisted mostly of a blacksmith forge and specialty woodworking equipment. Most of the woodwork was still done at Elizabeth's grandfather's shop, but because of the fear of fire, the blacksmith forge and specialty equipment were located in this building. The building was, in fact, fairly new, but this was mainly because the building routinely burned down every few years.

As Ezra walked in, he noticed how sooty things were and how strong the smell of the fire was. He thought this could not be a very pleasant place to work, especially during the hot, humid Maryland summers. Those thoughts passed quickly as he spied hundreds of blocks of all different sizes and configurations. They were constructed of both iron and wood. He surmised that the wood was either maple or oak for hardness and that the metal rings were forged from iron. Next to the blocks, in a large wooded barrel, were cleats like he had seen at the cookhouse, but of many sizes.

"Can I help you son?"

It was Old Mr. Jim addressing Ezra, who did not know what to say.

"I'm Ezra, my father is Mr. Pooles,"

"Yes son, I've seen you around the property. I knew who you were, but not your name."

"Yes sir, I just always wondered what you did here, I was just curious."

"Would you like me to show you around son?" Old Mr. Jim asked.

"Yes, Sir, that would be great," answered Ezra.

Old Mr. Jim showed him the forge first, as that was the real center of the operation. It was a large open pit raised above the floor and constructed of mortared rocks. Above the pit was a very large canopy made of some sort of metal, Ezra guessed tin. This canopy was used to try to direct some of the smoke from the coal pit through the roof of the building. Unfortunately, it was not very efficient, especially when Old Mr. Jim pushed the very large bellows, which was constructed of wood and leather, to cause the coals to glow red-hot. In the pit were several works in progress; in fact, Old Mr. Jim was working that day on cleats that were being forged in a row on a thin iron bar.

When he was pleased with their shape and size he would plunge the hot metal into a large barrel of water next to the pit. Ezra realized that the hot metal in the water was the source of the putrid odor that permeated the shop. He also was aware that Old Mr. Jim was what the boys referred to as "squirrelly," Ezra had no knowledge of the lead poisoning that inflicted Old Mr. Jim from his constant contact with that metal. He did know that all the boys feared him due to the sudden outbursts that seemed to come from nowhere. Today, however, Old Mr. Jim seemed fine, almost kind. Old Mr. Jim was still talking, but Ezra really was not listening. He was instead focused on the enormous number of implements hanging on the wall, many of which would meet their needs perfectly. The problem was that they were in this building that was occupied every day by workers who were under the constant eye of the "squirrelly" Old Mr. Jim and the workshop was locked every night due to the valuable devices that were created here.

Old Mr. Jim droned on.

"Well, you see here son," he said as he hit the bellows and a large puff of smoke engulfed Ezra and Old Mr. Jim. "We have to constantly be making these tools to be used all over the plantation. The things break all the time and we never know what will be needed next. They have to be ready when your old man, I'm sorry, that's Mr. Pooles requests them. So we just keep making them. Never figured out what or when, I guess we're just lucky. Hey you, back to work!"

One of Old Mr. Jim's famous outbursts was aimed at a very sweaty and obviously hard working slave next to the forge.

"Where were we? Oh yes, we have to keep way ahead of your old man, sorry, that's Mr. Pooles son."

Ezra noticed that the whole time he and Old Mr. Jim were talking that Old Mr. Jim puffed on a corncob pipe. Given the abundance of smoke in the building Ezra just could not understand how Old Mr. Jim received any enjoyment from the pipe. Old Mr. Jim wore half glasses that were perched in the tip of his nose. This gave him a rather menacing appearance, especially when talking to someone shorter than him, as Ezra was. Ezra thanked Old Mr. Jim and headed out to the creek bed glancing over his shoulder at the bounty of blocks. He now knew where, but not how, he would obtain them. This he would have to discuss with his co-workers.

Toby and Zeeney were already immersed in their work when Ezra arrived.

"Sleep in this morning?" They both chuckled.

"No, I took a tour of the location of the source for our blocks."

"Hope there's no water there!" Toby exclaimed.

"No water but also not easy. We have to get them out of there while Old Mr. Jim is there."

Toby and Zeeney collectively yelled, "Old Mr. Jim!"

"Or we'll have to figure a way into the building at night.

Both boys collectively screamed, "night!"

Chapter 6

T hey all decided they did not want to wait. Ezra had conveniently run into Elizabeth and found out that the masts and booms (tent poles) would be done by the end of the week. Being Tuesday, they did not want to hold off any longer. They wanted to have the blocks when the masts and sails arrived so that they could be rigged. Tonight was the night. That way if something went wrong they could regroup and do it another night. Collectively, they all wanted to complete this stage as soon as possible. Toby and Zeeney already feared Old Mr. Jim and Ezra's only meeting with him gave him pause as well. Tonight after supper it would be. They would meet on the south side of the workshop with lanterns and concoct their plan. It was usually dark around eight o'clock this time of year. Ezra could not be out after nine-thirty unless he had an excuse. It was too late to make one, so he figured they had about an hour to get in, get the blocks, and get back home.

Supper was not very enjoyable, Anna May had out done herself, which was truly amazing given her limited resources, but Ezra had blocks on his mind. As the time approached, his nervousness increased, he did not think they would fail, but they could be caught and he had no alibi should that occur. Soon after supper Ezra rooted through the shed behind his house searching for a lantern that not only had oil but also a descent wick. He had several to choose from so he choose the three best because he had not really discussed this with Toby and

Zeeney, but he decided that backup was a good idea anyway. It was almost dark so Ezra headed over to the cookhouse to light his lantern and then ran as fast as he could toward the workshop with one lit and two unlit lanterns. He would light the other two when he met up with the boys. There was a small wooded area just south of the workshop that was where they were to meet and make their plan. When Ezra arrived, Toby and Zeeney were there and had already devised a plan.

While Ezra lit the other two lanterns Toby told him of their plan. Conveniently, there was a ladder behind the workshop. They judged that this ladder would just meet a window on the back of the workshop. Toby knew from the times he had worked there that this window was in a loft area at the rear of the building. This loft overlooked the forge area and there was a ladder connected to the wall at the front of the loft. They would climb through the loft area down to the area where the blocks were, choose at least two appropriate blocks, and backtrack to leave the building. If it went as planned it would be easy. The boys took off running, being careful not to extinguish their lanterns. The ladder just reached, the window was unlocked. So far so good. They quickly climbed through the window and into the jumbled loft, it was fairly well packed with disorganized stacks of some sort of bales wrapped in burlap. As Ezra surveyed the disarray, looking for a path to get down to the lower level, he wondered what genius decided to store these bales up here. One spark from the forge and good-bye workshop. But that was not his problem. He wanted to get their blocks and be back home before nine-thirty. They quickly maneuvered through the maze. There did not seem to be any organization in the loft. It was as if the bales were just tossed from below and allowed to fall where they may. At the end of the open loft was a thin, roughly built ladder, attached to the wall. It was difficult and at first frightening to mount the ladder because they had to place one hand on a rung and then swing their bodies onto the ladder. This was actually easier than it appeared and they were quickly down the ladder and onto the floor where their prizes awaited.

Old Mr. Jim was taking his usual evening walk before retiring. He usually walked on the other side of the property, away from the workshop. He had worked in that building, in its various forms, for over twenty years. By the end of each day, he had enough of the building, the slaves, and especially the forge, and there was only so much yelling a man could do. This evening however he was not quite sure whether he had locked the large swinging doors that were the main access to the building. He did not know why he had been so forgetful lately, but attributed it to old age.

What else could it be?

As he approached the workshop he was keenly aware that something was amiss. There was usually a glow from the forge through the small windows on the side of the workshop as the forge was always burning, but tonight it was different. Instead of a steady glow, these lights flickered as if they moved around the workshop floor. As Old Mr. Jim arrived at the swinging doors, trying to be as quiet as possible, he reached for the lock. His night vision was slowly diminishing as he aged. When he felt the lock, he was surprised to discover it was in place. He first rattled the lock, shouted several salty words, and then fumbled for the key.

"What was that?" exclaimed Toby.

Ezra was the first to react. He was close to the barrel of cleats while Toby and Zeeney had headed directly to the front of the building where the blocks hung on the wall. Since Ezra was still very close to the ladder, he flew up the rungs, quickly followed by Toby and Zeeney.

Zeeney whispered to Toby, "Douse your light," which they both did quickly. This put them well behind Ezra who was already up in the loft and, they assumed, through the window to safety. As the doors swung opened Old Mr. Jim yelled, " Who's there?"

Toby and Zeeney had never gone up a ladder so fast in their lives. When they reached the top, they leaped onto the loft. Zeeney, being last, almost misjudged the distance and would have fallen to the floor had not the quick reflexes of Toby saved the day. Although it was now completely dark, their young eyes had adjusted and they could clearly see their exit route through the window. Old Mr. Jim was not as fortunate. As he could barely see in the low light conditions, all he could see were shapes. He stumbled through the workshop falling several times. Each time he arose he would yell, "Stop thief!"

The more he yelled the faster the boys ran. Toby thought that Ezra was not as fast as them, but on this night he must be faster. He was nowhere to be seen. The boys almost leaped through the window and stumbled down the ladder. They quickly pulled the ladder from the window and ran at lightning speed back to the wooded area.

When they collapsed back at the clearing where they first planned their game of attack, Ezra was not there. Had he been so frightened that he had just kept running all the way home? If not, where was he? The boys decided that the best plan of action was to wait to see who their pursuer was.

Meanwhile, back in the workshop, Old Mr. Jim still fumbled in the dark. He finally found a lantern, which he quickly lit, and was relieved to be able to see again. He approached the ladder and did not relish the idea of climbing it, especially with a lighted lantern in his hand. He slowly ascended the ladder. As he reached the top, he wondered, "How in the world am I going to get onto that loft?" When he realized that any attempt would be life threatening, he decided instead to climb to the top of the ladder and use the lantern to see the perpetrators. They were not going anywhere, as there was no exit from the loft, or so he thought. When he reached the very top he could clearly see the bright opening that was the thieves point of departure. The window on the south wall was wide open. After many expletives, Old Mr. Jim slowly descended the ladder. He would not catch them tonight. He walked through the swinging doors and toward the rear of the building where the perpetrators had exited. When he arrived at the back, he discovered the ladder on the ground not far from the back of the building. He looked up and lifted the lantern high to illuminate the open window. Tomorrow the ladder would be removed and the window nailed shut! No one was stealing from Old Mr. Jim!

Toby and Zeeney could clearly see Old Mr. Jim illuminated by his lantern. They were frightened and completely forgot about Ezra, thinking he must be tucked into his bed by now.

"Should we run Zeeney?" asked Toby.

"I don't know. Let's see what Old Mr. Jim does," Zeeney replied.

They did not have to wait long. Old Mr. Jim headed back to the doors and briefly inside the building to see what was missing. He was not aware of any missing items, although it was difficult, to be sure, with the myriad of items throughout the workshop; apparently he had discovered the thieves before they completed their thievery. He would lock the doors and continue his walk, but he would come back this way to confirm that they did not return.

Old Mr. Jim locked up and continued on his way lighting his pipe as he walked and muttered more expletives about what exactly he would do to the thieves if he should catch them. This brought a huge smile to Old Mr. Jim's face.

He walked quickly away, still muttering. Toby and Zeeney watched his departure with great relief. They would wait several minutes before leaving because Old Mr. Jim had chosen the direction that they lived in which to head. If he were to double back, they would be caught for sure. They decided to wait even longer and it was a good thing they did.

Chapter 7

Ezra was not in bed, in fact he was nowhere near his home. As he pushed the light bale out of the way, he headed over to the window to exit. As he had jumped from the loft ladder in his haste, he had hit his knee on the beam that supported the loft, rendering him temporarily disabled. Since he could no longer run, he felt that concealment was his best option. He quickly pulled the light bales over his body to conceal himself. He thought his plan had failed when he saw Toby and Zeeney rush by. He was convinced that their pursuer was hot on their trail and, at the very least, would trip over him. He did not yell out to Toby and Zeeney because he knew it would reveal his position. He was still in too much pain to accompany them, so he decided to stay in place. He was sure he was caught as Old Mr. Jim stood at the top of the loft ladder merely feet from where Ezra was concealed. Ezra could clearly see Mr. Jim through the cracks in the hastily thrown bales, and he could clearly hear the words he muttered. Although shaking with fear, Ezra was nonetheless fascinated by the vocabulary of words he had never heard before that night. He thought that they could be very useful to him in the future.

As he heard the doors swing shut and the large padlock click in place, he felt somewhat relieved. He still had to get out safely in case someone returned. He ran to the window and was about to leap when, at the last possible second, he noticed that the ladder was gone. What would he do now? He had no idea where Toby and Zeeney were but assumed that if they had gotten safely away, they had kept right on running. They were so afraid of Old Mr. Jim that they were not going to hang around if they could get safely away. He was doomed! Early the next morning he would try to sneak out but he knew that Old Mr. Jim or one of the workers would notice him and know that he was the thief that Old Mr. Jim had unsuccessfully pursued the night before.. He would not be able to explain why he was in the building. He was also aware that for lesser transgressions, he had been punished severely. His father was a very stern man, and Ezra knew that any chance of finishing the boat and starting on his adventure with Toby and Zeeney had just vanished. Ezra would sleep in the loft that night and then turn himself in to Old Mr. Jim the next morning. He would say that his earlier visit had made him more curious and he wanted to find out more about the workshop. As he stood there staring out the window, he knew that no one would believe his story. Old Mr. Jim would turn him in to his father and that his father would put him on restriction for the entire summer. Surely, he was doomed!

Just as Ezra started back to the bales to find an appropriate place to sleep that night, he saw movement at the edge of the woods. He could not see clearly as they were just a shape but he immediately decided to take a chance. If it was Old Mr. Jim doubling back, he would be caught, but he figured that being caught was a foregone conclusion. He would definitely be caught the next morning. If it was Toby and Zeeney, who he was sure were long gone, there was an outside chance he might still escape. He took a chance. He turned up the wick on the lantern and swung it outside the window. Immediately the shape changed direction and headed toward Ezra. He swallowed deeply.

As the shadow approached it was clear that there were two shapes, not one. It probably was not Old Mr. Jim, but he was not sure that it was definitely Toby and Zeeney either. Closer and closer the shapes came. When almost at the building, Ezra was extremely relieved to see that it was, in fact, his friends and not his potential captor.

He yelled down to them in a whisper, "Please get me out of here!"

"What happened," Toby asked.

"I fell down and hurt myself, I hid."

"Did Old Mr. Jim see you?" asked Zeeney.

"No I don't think so otherwise he would have come after me."

"Are you alright now?" asked Toby.

"Yes, thanks, I just want to get out of here."

"Alright, we'll put the ladder back up for you," replied Toby.

As Toby and Zeeney approached the ladder and just before they picked it up, Ezra exclaimed, "Leave the ladder alone, I don't want to come down yet."

Both Toby and Zeeney exclaimed, in unison, "What? Are you crazy?"

Ezra explained, "If we fail tonight, it will be the second time we failed. I am out of ideas on how we will come up with the blocks and cleats if we don't get them tonight. After tonight Old Mr. Jim is liable to put a guard in here and we'll never get another chance. It is now or never."

Both Toby and Zeeney yelled in a whisper, "We're not coming back in that building!"

"You don't have to," replied Ezra. "Leave the ladder where it is and head back to the woods. I'll signal you from this window once I have what we came for. You two keep an eye out for Old Mr. Jim or anyone else that might happen by. When you see my lantern and everything looks good, signal me with both your lanterns. Then run as fast as you can and put the ladder up and we're out of here."

Toby and Zeeney dimmed their lanterns, as did Ezra. Ezra had noticed that while laying in the bales that his eyes had become quite accustomed to the faint glow of the forge. He could not take a chance of lighting the lantern again as he was sure that this was the reason Old Mr. Jim knew there was someone in the workshop before he opened the large doors. Ezra waited about five minutes before he proceeded. He could see quite well by now, but still moved cautiously. He did not want to trip and injure himself again. He decided to leave the lantern by the window, as he would not need it again until it was time to signal Toby and Zeeney. He was off.

The only thing he carried now was the satchel that he brought originally to carry his booty. When he got back to the ladder, he was again very cautious to swing onto the ladder without falling. A broken leg would only add to the misery of being punished. He decided on the way down the ladder that his main goal was the blocks and that he would go for them first. He surmised that the blocks were the immediate requirement and, if he had to beat a hasty retreat, at the very least he might have the blocks. His nervousness almost overcame his joy as he stood in front of the wall of blocks. He examined them and noticed immediately that they were in a random pattern of size and function. This he felt was a good thing because it would be very easy to disguise their disappearance. Unfortunately, his joy immediately disappeared. With more detailed inspection, he noticed that there indeed was a pattern, and unfortunately for him it was quite organized He also decided that, after all the trouble they had gone to, he would get a minimum of six similar blocks instead of two and then at least two combination blocks. He would try to find combination blocks about the same size of the single blocks. This way he would be covering future needs he might possibly be overlooking. He knew well that he could not take the blocks and leave empty spaces. That would surely set Old Mr.

Jim into a rage and cause his father to send out a group of his workers to find the stolen property and the thieves connected with them. How could he take the blocks without anyone knowing? The cleats, "he thought," would be easy. They were in a jumble in the barrel and could be easily disguised. But what was he to do about the blocks?

Ezra knew that the time for his departure had come and gone. He would have to think very fast. He started by observing the wall. He still had parchment and lumps of coal in his satchel, so he thought there had to be a plan that would deceive Old Mr. Jim. Ezra remembered what Old Mr. Jim had told him during his tour.

"We have to constantly be making these tools to be used all over the plantation. The things break all the time and we never know what will be needed next. Since they have to be ready when your old man, I'm sorry, that's Mr. Pooles, requests them, we just keep making them."

So as "squirrelly" as Old Mr. Jim was, he had a pretty good system of knowing what was missing and had to be made next. Now Ezra had a problem, for he would be all night rearranging the wall to disguise the theft. He felt that Old Mr. Jim could probably look up on that wall and immediately know what was missing. Since there were intruders that Old Mr. Jim almost caught, he would surely press for an investigation on the plantation. Ezra would be found out and disciplined just the same or possible worse. He had heard that in some colonies thieves were branded with a "T" he certainly did not want to go through life with that on his face.

Just as he was thinking, he turned toward the forge and noticed a long rod against the forge wall. It had in the shape of a "T" at the end.

Ezra squealed, "Yikes! Time to get to work!"

Although there was no time. Ezra had to be at home and in bed at nine-thirty and he was sure it was quickly approaching that time. His reasons for being punished were stacking up quickly.

In looking at the wall of blocks, Ezra wrote down some basic information. There were pegs covering almost the entire wall but not all in use. All the blocks where bunched together in a symmetrical, rectangular pattern. It was obvious to Ezra that this wall had been used for quite some time for this purpose and that the system must have changed many times as there were ghost patterns of blocks on the wall where the unused pegs were. Ezra started counting. There were seven horizontal rows stacked up the wall and each row had exactly forty items. There were some blank spots, but not many. Ezra knew he could not simply take the blocks, as that would be entirely too easy for Old Mr.Jim to notice. He was sure this was Old Mr. Jim's creation because, as far as Ezra knew, Old Mr. Jim was the only person who had ever run the workshop. Ezra got to work. He scribbled on his parchment a basic diagram of the wall. He assigned numbers to each type of block. There were three. Coincidentally, the first block at the beginning of the top row was the basic block he was seeking, so he assigned that block as number one. That row began and ended with the same block and then the next row started with the second block, number 2, and the third row with the third block, number 3. This pattern repeated for a total of seven rows, a lot of blocks. Ezra used these numbers to create a diagram of the wall:

1231231231231231231231231231231231231231
2312312312312312312312312312312312312312
3123123123123123123123123123123123123123
1231231231231231231231231231231231231231
2312312312312312312312312312312312312312
3123123123123123123123123123123123123123
1231231231231231231231231231231231231231

Ezra looked at the diagram for some time and he decided to eliminate the entire last row. He would then fill in the pattern at the end of each row with some of the blocks, that would surely leave him with all the blocks he would need. He devised this plan:

1231231231231231231231231231231231231231231
2312312312312312312312312312312312312312312
3123123123123123123123123123123123123123123
1231231231231231231231231231231231231231231
2312312312312312312312312312312312312312312
3123123123123123123123123123123123123123123

Taking away the entire bottom row gave Ezra forty blocks to work with. He laid them on the dirt floor in piles of 1-2-3. He then started adding to the end of each row to complete the pattern. At the end of the top row he added 2-3-1, to the second row 3-1-2. He repeated this pattern until all rows were complete. It looked pretty good to Ezra. Not only was it symmetrical and repeated the pattern properly, it left him with more blocks than he originally intended. Lying on the dirt floor were three piles of blocks, eight number 1's, five number 2's, and five number 3's. It was more than he intended to take but he felt this was the best plan and would give him plenty of spare parts should they fail. Ezra was feeling pretty good about himself.

"Zeeney couldn't have come up with a better plan," he muttered out loud.

Quickly he moved back toward the ladder and the barrel of cleats. This would be easy, he would just grab about ten of the cleats and jumble the remaining cleats to make the appearance of the same volume. In the satchel they went. Ezra noticed that the satchel was now quite heavy. Over to the ladder he ran, but just before he was to ascend the ladder, he spied stacks of freshly made rope. He quickly grabbed one long coil, placed it on his shoulder, and then leaped back on the ladder ascending as fast as the heavy satchel would allow. At the top he swung the satchel onto the loft and jumped, this time being careful not to hit his knee on the beam as he had done earlier. He could still remember the pain. He moved quickly toward the window, grabbing and turning the lantern wick up in almost one swift motion. He then looked below the window to make sure that no one was approaching. He saw that everything seemed fine, so he reached for and swung the lantern from the window. Almost immediately he saw not one, but two lanterns illuminate from the wooded clearing behind the workshop. He was relieved but it was not over.

Toby and Zeeney nervously waited in the clearing. Ezra had been in the workshop far longer than they had anticipated. They were getting more fretful as time passed. Maybe Ezra had fallen and hurt himself or maybe Old Mr. Jim came back, snuck in another entrance and captured Ezra. What were they going to do? When they finally saw Ezra's signal light they were overjoyed. They leaped to their feet after extinguishing the lanterns, they wanted to be as invisible as they possibly could. The distance between the wooded clearing was not all that far, but to Toby and Zeeney it seemed to take forever. They ran to the ladder, dropped the lanterns and quickly placed the ladder against the wall beneath the window. Out flew Ezra with the heavy satchel. He more slid down the ladder than climbed. When he hit the ground, the ladder was quickly pulled down and placed approximately where it was originally. They were off in a gallop, Ezra to his home, and Toby and Zeeney to their homes.

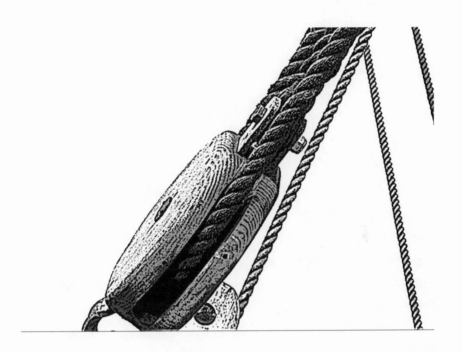

Basic Sailing Block

Illustration by Tom Scheuerman

Chapter 8

Ezra was flying. Even with the heavy satchel he was making great time. As he approached his house he saw an encouraging sign, there was no candlelight in his room. He ran quickly to his window trying to control his breathing. He raised the window, threw the satchel through it and climbed through trying to be as quiet as possible. He tossed the satchel under his bed and jumped into bed. He had no idea what time it was, but it had to be well after nine-thirty. He still had his clothes on but pulled the covers up over them in case anyone checked on him. He had to control his breathing. He wiped the sweat off repeatedly. As he lay there he started to calm down and reflect on the adventure he had just completed. He was very excited. They were ahead of schedule, and the masts and booms would be done by Friday. He decided to try to run into Elizabeth and at least get an update on the tent cover. Was this going too smoothly? As he contemplated his next move, he heard a knock at the door, and then it opened. It was his mother.

Emily Pooles was rather progressive for her time, Ezra was her fourth of six children and she did not like to restrain either their freedom or their creativity. The only thing she demanded was that they obey her rules. She had not seen her son all day or night and had just finished tucking in the two younger children. It was now approaching ten o'clock and she checked on Ezra just to make sure everything was all right. She had a small candelabra in her left hand that contained three beeswax candles.

"How are you son?" She said in a whispering voice.

Ezra replied, "Oh, I'm fine mother, just going to sleep."

"We haven't seen you since early this morning. In fact, we didn't even see you come in tonight."

"You didn't. I walked right in the back door from the rear porch. I could hear you talking to Jeremy, but didn't want to disturb you, I was tired and came right to bed. I've been working hard, you know, clearing the creek bed for Father. I just wanted to get some sleep."

"Well that's a good thing dear, get your sleep. Your father told me this evening how proud he was of you. He said you are single handedly supervising two slaves in the clearing of the creek bed. In fact, he's coming by there tomorrow to check your progress. He's so proud. Get some sleep son."

Chapter 9

Old Mr. Jim was never eager to start work, but he had done it so long it was like breathing. When he arrived, his workers had already prepared the projects for the day. Old Mr. Jim walked in and started into immediate rant.

"Did any of them thieving so and sos steal anything?"

Joshua, one of the oldest and most trusted, said, "Boss, what are you talking about?"

Old Mr. Jim told Joshua what had happened the night before.

"Yes, I almost caught them, the thieving #*&%@. Let me know what the #*&%@ stole."

Joshua rolled his eyes. Old Mr. Jim worried everybody that worked in the workshop but not Joshua. Joshua knew that Old Mr. Jim would not complete most of the projects on time without Joshua's help. More importantly, he knew that Old Mr. Jim knew it as well. Joshua tolerated Old Mr. Jim. He had known him before he had become "squirrelly." At one time, he had liked Old Mr. Jim, but that probably was when he was just Mr. Jim. Joshua was a very hard worker and planned most of the schedule for the workshop. He had devised the new system for storing the blocks as Old Mr. Jim's system just did not work. It was a jumbled mess and they were always making an abundance of blocks they did not need. Joshua took on the project of revising the wall where the blocks were stored. He came up with a simple numerical system that repeated as blocks were pulled, no matter which one or what quantity, his system would have complete redundancy. They could now easily check which blocks were to be made next. Joshua knew his system was good, especially the day that Mr. Pooles came to visit to see how things were progressing at the workshop.

Mr. Pooles walked into the workshop fairly late in the morning. He was very interested in the new system that Old Mr. Jim had devised to eliminate the recurring problem they had on the plantation. Blocks that were used for various projects were not available when needed, and sometimes days would pass before the workshop delivered the blocks needed to finish a project. Mr. Pooles was not happy and told Old Mr. Jim that either the system needed to changed or Old Mr. Jim could walk to Baltimore town to seek future employment. Old Mr. Jim would stare at the wall where the blocks were stored, but day after day he could not come up with a solution. One day Joshua came to Old Mr. Jim and asked if he could take over the wall and devise a system to store the blocks. He had become quite tired of Old Mr. Jim staring at the wall, but make no progress.

"All right, you horse's ass, the wall is yours, but if you fail I will personally beat the tar out of you. I'm not starting a new job because you don't know what the %#* you're doing!"

Joshua already had a plan in his mind. He had devised it months ago, but had never brought it to Old Mr. Jim. Everyone that worked at the workshop knew that the only good ideas were Old Mr. Jim's ideas. When Joshua started his wall project, he knew that it would take weeks to complete. He already had the solution, but knew that if he completed it too fast Old Mr. Jim would either punish him for being uppity or just give him the nastiest jobs in the workshop. How could an ignorant slave come up with a system that Old Mr. Jim could not? So every day Joshua would come to the workshop and just stare at the wall. He did this for a week. When Old Mr. Jim would take breaks from his work schedule, he would come to the wall and stand next to Joshua.

Sometimes he would even put his arm around Joshua's shoulder and say, "Son, I know how hard this is, especially for darkies, but you just keep trying, Son.

Joshua could only answer, "Yes, Sir, I'm trying Sir."

The next morning when Old Mr. Jim arrived at the workshop Joshua had his system in place with the blocks up on the wall. He explained the he used a 1-2-3 system because those were the blocks that were always used on the plantation. They could be pulled from any place on the wall in any order, but as long as the blanks were replaced with newly manufactured blocks, they would never run out and, even better, never upset Mr. Pooles. Since the system continued 1-2-3 from beginning to end, they would never have to rearrange the wall, just take a list of the blank spaces to schedule the next manufacturing run. It was both simple and functional. This would give the workers all the time they needed to manufacture the replacements without making too many of the wrong items, or too few of the right ones. The system quickly became Old Mr. Jim's system.

Chapter 10

As Mr. Pooles entered the workshop, Old Mr. Jim dropped the rods he was working on and ran quickly over to him, practically bowing as he removed his hat. He behaved as if the King of England was arriving. Old Mr. Jim was anxious to show Mr. Pooles the system he had devised to assure there would be no more work stoppages due to not having the required blocks. He also informed Mr. Pooles of the previous night's intruder. He explained that they got away, but only after he ran them clear off the property. Mr. Pooles thought they must have been some very feeble thieves for Old Mr. Jim to run them off. As he took Mr. Pooles to the wall to explain "his" new system, he asked Joshua what was missing from the shop.

"Sir, as best as we can tell, nothing, but we is still looking. Looks like you run them off before they could steal anything."

"Thank you Joshua, that will be all."

"Well, as I was saying, I call it the 1-2-3 system, because those are the blocks most frequently used. We can now easily see what is needed, you'll never hear about us running out again."

Joshua interrupted. "Boss, that isn't right!"

Old Mr. Jim quickly scanned the wall, "Starts with 1, ends with 3, he counted 1-2-3-1-2-3-1-2-3.... 1-2-3-1-2-3, down the left, 1-2-3-1-2-3, down the right. What the %#*@#s wrong with it? You get back to work, you lazy &#@*#, and don't tell me about my system. I designed it. I sure as #&@%# would know if it's wrong. Now get back to work before I give you a beating."

Again Joshua shook his head, and muttered to himself. "Wonder what they're going to do with all them blocks?"

As Mr. Pooles was leaving, Old Mr. Jim said, "Oh, by the way I met your son yesterday, fine boy, fine boy."

"Oh, which one?" Mr. Pooles replied, I have four sons."

"He was a young one. I think he said his name was Ester."

"Ezra," said Mr. Pooles.

"Yes sir, that was his name. Fine boy, fine boy."

"How did you meet him?" Mr. Pooles asked.

"Well, he came by to get a tour of the workshop. Seems he didn't know what we did here and he was curious."

Mr. Pooles was surprised. He had never known Ezra to be curious about anything on the plantation. Most of his curiosity was aimed at figuring ways to get himself and those two slave boys he ran with, Toby and Zeeney, out of work. Mr. Pooles knew that would change on Ezra's upcoming 13th birthday because he would start assigning him real jobs on the plantation. Even the creek bed clearing was a good test to see how he handled responsibility and the delegation of duties. Jeremiah was very surprised that Ezra had volunteered for anything. He was further surprised by Ezra's "curiosity" about the workshop. Mr. Pooles looked to the ground and smiled.

"Maybe my boy is becoming a man all by himself," he thought.

"Coincidentally Jim, I'm on my way to see my son Ezra at this very moment. He has taken on a very important project. I want to see the progress he and his crew have made and tell him how proud I am of his manly actions."

"Well, you give him my regards," Old Mr. Jim said. "Fine boy, fine boy."

Old Mr. Jim staggered away from Mr. Pooles. All Mr. Pooles heard as Old Mr. Jim re-entered the workshop was."Fine boy, fine boy," interspersed with #%&# yelled at each worker he passed.

Chapter 11

Ezra was running as fast as he did the night before, maybe faster. He had to get to the creek bed before his father did. If his father found the felled tree and the rough boat that the boys had started to create, his goose was cooked! As he ran he tried to remember how much work they had done on the creek bed. With all the things that had taken place in the last couple days he really wasn't sure how much he had accomplished. He was surprised that his father would be checking on him, especially this early in the project. Ezra's father never checked on him, especially at one of the busiest times of the year.

When Ezra arrived at the creek bed and looked up toward the rise where the boat was, all he could see of Toby and Zeeney were their backsides. As he got closer, he saw that they were working, side-by-side, chiseling the interior of the boat smooth. He knew what painstaking work this was. Any other time he would be appreciative, but not today.

"Drop everything!" he yelled. This startled both Toby and Zeeney and they immediately dropped the chisels inside the boat.

"What's wrong? Is Old Mr. Jim after us?"

"No even worse! My father's on his way here to check on the work we have done."

"When," chimed Toby.

" I don't know," replied Ezra. "It could be anytime. We have to hide this boat and make the creek bed look like we have been working hard."

Toby and Zeeney both looked down at the boat.

"How are we going to hide it, and what about the satchel?"

Ezra had forgotten all about the satchel. He had another project and very little time.

He looked around the area. The creek bed was below them, and he saw some small piles of debris they had made on previous days. Each pile was not much, but he thought that as one larger pile, it might just work. He threw the satchel in the boat.

"Oh, that's a good hiding spot," Toby chuckled.

"If Father finds the boat it won't really matter what he finds inside, we're cooked! We'll just have to hide it well enough to keep him from seeing it."

Toby and Zeeney started to laugh, even though their situation was not humorous.

"We can't move this boat, it's too heavy. How are we going to keep him from finding it? We might as well lay back, take a nap, and wait till we're busted because that sure enough is what is going to happen."

"No!" Ezra exclaimed. "We can hide it. Let's start by bringing the piles of debris up here. There aren't many, but maybe enough to cover the boat."

"How about that big thing there?" Zeeney pointed to the felled tree.

"How we gonna hide that, with magic? Last time I heard Mr. Pooles don't like nobody chopping trees down on his property, but Mr. Pooles. How we gonna hide that?"

Ezra quickly ran down to the creek bed. When he arrived there he turned and look back at the rise. Although clearly visible from the creek bed, Ezra felt that if they stacked enough debris around the boat it might also obscure the tree because the tree was directly behind the boat. Unfortunately, it was on a slight angle, which did not help. They would just have to keep Mr. Pooles and whatever workers he had with him at the creek bed. If he approached anywhere near the rise he would spot the tree, then, of course, he would most likely find the boat. There was nothing they could say to explain the felled tree and the rough boat, especially with so little time

"Quick!" he said. "Let's get to work." We haven't much time."

The boys started to grab piles of debris and rush them up to the rise. They were careful not to compress the piles as they stacked them loosely in front the boat. They wanted as much volume as possible, especially with the limited amount of debris they had to work with.

Ezra was thinking, "We should have devoted more time to the creek bed. Then we would have enough to do the job."

They had just finished the last pile when they heard the sound of men, horses, and a carriage off in the distance. Ezra knew there was little time and if father got anywhere near the rise, the debris pile would peek his curiosity and he would approach it.

He yelled to Toby and Zeeney, "Quick, there are some large ferns in the uncleared part of the creek bed. Run as fast as you can, get as many as possible and bring them up here. I'll run to the top of the rise to see if there are any fallen tree limbs. Hurry, it's our only chance!"

Ezra ran up the hill as Toby and Zeeney ran down, the sound of the horses was intensifying. Mr. Pooles and his men would be approaching from the creek itself as the only dirt road that gave access to the creek bed ran along the creek. This would give the boys only minutes after the men dismounted before they were in the creek bed area. Ezra knew that he, Toby and Zeeney had to be in the creek bed when they arrived, otherwise the men might head up the rise looking for Ezra. That would be a disaster! Ezra, Toby and Zeeney all arrived at the boat at the same time. They were each carrying their maximum capacity. Ezra started but Toby quickly followed tossing debris on the pile.

"No!" Ezra yelled. "Let me get my tree limbs on the stack then you can follow with the ferns, stack them as carefully as you can to conceal. This might just work! After I get the limbs down, I'll head to the creek bed. I'll try to divert their attention away from this area. As soon as you finish, run back to the creek bed and keep an eye on Father's men. We don't want any curiosity."

Ezra arrived seconds before his father and his men strolled into the creek bed. Mr. Pooles had a pair of riding gloves in his right hand, which he used to strike his left hand. Ezra did not know what to make of this. Was he angry and just about to rip into Ezra?

What Ezra did not know is that it was a nervous habit of his father's. He did it as a diversion when he did not know what he was about to say. On this day he had the added burden of not knowing what to expect of his son's project.

"Father!" Ezra exclaimed. "Welcome to the creek bed!"

Ezra forced the biggest smile he could conjure. He was very relieved when he heard Toby and Zeeney stumble down the rise to the creek bed. He was going to need their help to divert attention away from the debris pile.

"Hello Mr. Pooles sir," Toby and Zeeney said in unison.

"Well it appears that you boys have been working hard. Look how dirty and sweaty you all are, I bet you all have worked up enormous appetites."

"Oh, yes sir," they all said at once.

"Well give me the tour, son."

"Yes sir," the obedient Ezra replied. Out of the corner of his eye Ezra spotted one of father's men wandering toward the rise.

"Toby," he yelled, "why don't you take father's men down where we catch the big bass down by the creek?"

Zeeney looked over to Ezra.

"What bass down by the creek?" he thought.

"Yes, boss," was his reply to Ezra. Although they decided that they were partners, they had to put on the disguise that Ezra was running this operation. Zeeney did not know exactly what to do, but he and Toby quickly herded the much larger men away from the creek bed and toward the creek itself.

"You see Father, here is my plan. We will remove as much ground cover from the creek bed as possible, leaving the area for any project you instruct me to do."

"Oh, yes," father replied. " I did not tell you what was to come of this area once you have it cleared, I probably should have told you earlier, but after all it was your idea to clear the area, not mine"

"Yes sir," Ezra beamed.

"I would like to build a dock in the creek, over at the high point of the shoreline, and use this area to construct a few small fishing boats to be used in the creek. I think this would be a perfect area to work on such a project, especially with the abundance of trees in the area."

Ezra was in complete shock and for once in his young life speechless, he was also very confused. Throughout his entire existence, all his parents would ever say about the Chesapeake Bay was how dangerous it was. He and his siblings had constant reminders of the death of Zachary, especially anytime they were near the water. Now his father was ordering Ezra to build the very object that he had learned was forbidden.

"Father, I'm confused! You and mother have always told me how dangerous boats are, especially on the bay. Now you want me to build a boatyard?"

Ezra's father laughed, "Sorry, son, I guess I am giving you a confusing order. I have been think about this for quite sometime. It has been almost eleven years since Zachary passed away. I know we have preached to you and your brothers and sister how truly dangerous the water can be, but a lot of time has passed and I have decided that I have given you all the wrong message. Son, Zachary died because he had no real fear of the bay, he was not a strong swimmer, and no one had the opportunity to teach him anything about boating safety. He and his foolish friends went off and built a boat without my knowledge. By the time I found out, it was too late. Yes, now is the time to build a boatyard and boats, but before any of the family uses any of them they will be properly taught and know how to deal with the dangers of the bay. Also, all I want now are simple fishing boats that will float on this creek, more elaborate vessels will come later."

As he made this startling revelation to Ezra, he started to scan the horizon up on the rise. Ezra could not believe his ears. They truly were father and son. Maybe someday in the distant future Ezra would tell this story to his father over an ale. Then Ezra looked up and saw his father's eyes scanning the horizon.

"Father, that's a great idea! Please let me show you what I've done over here!" He practically yelled to divert his father's attention.

"Oh yes son, please show me what you have come up with."

"This way," Ezra said as he tried to figure out exactly what it was he was about to show his father.

He just kept leading his father farther and farther away from the rise. He did not know how Toby and Zeeney were doing with their "fish story." He just hoped they were resourceful enough to keep the men occupied. Ezra led his father to a debris pile they had missed. This was not much, but it was all he had

"You see Father, we clear an area then tote the debris pile up to the rise. When we're all done I'm planning a large bonfire."

Mr. Pooles said, "Ezra, do you think that is wise given all the wood in that area. What about fire, Son? Why don't we go to the rise next and I'll determine if it is safe. You do remember the large brush fire we had last year that almost destroyed the lower half of the plantation?"

"Oh, yes sir," Ezra replied. "Bad idea."

"Well, let's go check it out anyway to get a lay of land." This was the worst possible thing his father could say. How would he keep Father off the rise?

As they walked in that direction, Ezra's brain was churning.

"You know what father? You are right, a bonfire on the rise is a bad idea. Why don't we just plan to drag everything down to the creek and burn it in smaller piles that we can control. You're right again Father."

As they approached the center of the creek bed, Ezra saw Toby and Zeeney approach with father's men. Then Mr. Pooles started with the glove slapping again, either a very good or very bad sign.

"Well men, it appears that my son has the situation under control. Let's let them get back to their chores."

Ezra was elated. They were going to succeed.

"Let's go men."

As the group of men started to leave the creek bed one of the men turned and pointed saying, "Look at that!"

They all turned to the area he was pointing, the debris pile and the tree. Ezra's heart sank. Then he saw a small fox run from behind the debris pile.

"Well, you don't usually see them critters running during the day. Fact is, you don't usually see them at all." The startled fox took off in the other direction.

Mr.Pooles said, "All right men, let's go. We have work to do as do these men."

Chapter 12

Toby and Zeeney followed the group of men back to their horses. As the men retreated, the two boys waved as they walked slowly in the cloud dust that rose behind the group of horses. When they saw the last horse make the turn at the point and disappear behind the tall trees that bordered the dirt road, they finally felt a moment of relief. Beyond all odds they had pulled it off. They had a chance now to continue the adventure. Neither of them wanted to think of the consequences that might have befell them had they been caught. They may have been separated from Ezra, who they loved as a brother, or given awful chores to complete for the rest of their lives. Fortunately, it did not happen and they were relieved.

As they turned and walked back to the creek bed, all they could hear was loud laughter. It was Ezra. He was lying in the middle of the creek bed staring straight up to the sky and laughing almost uncontrollably. Toby and Zeeney automatically decided that this was the consequence of the relief that Ezra must be feeling. Toby and Zeeney surrounded Ezra. His eyes were closed and tears were streaming down his cheeks as he continued to laugh. The boys grabbed Ezra's two arms and pulled him to a seated position.

"Ezra," Toby said, "what's so funny?"

Ezra tried to compose himself and answer, but every time he thought about the statement his father had made regarding the future of the creek bed, he laughed even harder.

"My father…, my father…, wants to…., my father wants to build…." He just started laughing again even harder.

"What does your father want to build?" pleaded Zeeney.

"A boatyard!" spurted Ezra. With that, Toby and Zeeney made eye contact and erupted into enough laughter to equal Ezra's. They fell down laughing next to Ezra. As one boy would finally stop laughing, one of the other boys would start back up. It was so contagious that, at one point, Ezra thought they would never stop. His sides were actually starting to ache from the activity. Eventually the laughter began to die, although there were a few chuckles that almost started them to repeat their laugh fest.

As they sat there smiling at each other Ezra made a statement.

"First of all, I can't believe Father wants a boatyard built here. Little does he know he already has one."

They all started again, but this time Ezra raised his hands for them to stop.

"We have to come up with a better plan for the boat. Surely Father will be back. We can't go through this every time."

"But you just said Mr. Pooles wants us to build a boatyard. Why can't we just tell him about the boat? " asked Zeeney.

"Well," Ezra replied, "My father wants small fishing boats built for the creek, not a sailing vessel like the one we are building for the bay. No, we will have to continue to build it in secrecy, otherwise father will demand that we not use the boat until he has completed his safety course. We are committed to our adventure and I don't want to wait, it could be next year, or longer, before he would allow us to even use it."

"It's funny, but as soon as Father mentioned a boatyard, I pictured our boat floating in the water next to the creek."

"You mean in the creek," Toby chimed in.

"No, next to it. We can dig a trench on the creek shore to a depth slightly more than the boat, then allow the creek to flood it."

"Alright," Toby asked, "how do we get the boat from the rise to the creek? It's still to heavy for us to push."

"I already thought of that, Zeeney gave me the answer before we started. Plow horse!"

"Plow horse!" Toby and Zeeney replied. "Where are we going to get a plow horse?"

Ezra continued, "It's easier now that we don't have to use deception and lies anymore, especially the thieving. I really didn't like the thieving."

"How did you come up with that?" said Toby. "Just a few seconds ago, we were planning how to hide the boat we didn't make, and now, no problem, we are going to come up with a plow horse, and end all deception and thieving?"

"Simple," Ezra replied, "Father just gave us the license. No matter what we need in the future we just state that it is for the boatyard project Father ordered. After we tell enough people everyone will believe it. Now, we've wasted enough time. Let's go get our masts and booms. We have a boat to build!"

Chapter 13

Ezra knew that the three boys could not handle much more excitement. Their adventure had not really started and already, one had nearly drowned, they had been chased, cursed at, and pulled off a last minute deception. They needed a break. He decided to slow down the pace and figure out what they should do next without rushing anything. There were many pieces of their adventure puzzle yet to be completed. They had time, but Ezra wanted to create a more structured plan, more structured, that is, than the one they had currently. Which was, in fact, no plan at all. He vowed to himself that when he met with Toby and Zeeney, instead of just doing what they had so far, devising a real plan was the next thing that needed to be done. He would suggest they spend most of that day creating a schedule. He needed only to remind the boys of Father's visit yesterday. He knew if another occurrence happened similar to the day before, they would not fair as well.

When Ezra arrived at the creek bed, he viewed the same sight he had seen on arrivals days before, Toby and Ezra's backsides. He thought, maybe if we change things and do not start each day this way, we might have better luck. He brought another satchel with him this morning, but instead of containing blocks, cleats and rope, this one contained some of Anna May's delicious creations. Ezra thought planning would be easier if they had some delicious food to go with it. He also brought two jars of sweet tea for the boys to share.

"Why don't we take a break and go to the shed?" Ezra offered. "Anna May gave me some of her lamb stew and turnips for us to eat. It's still warm. I also brought some sweet tea."

Toby and Zeeney needed no other encouragement, although they had just eaten about an hour earlier. These boys would eat whenever food was offered, especially anything made by Anna May. They both dropped their hammers and chisels and headed for the shed.

When they arrived at the shed, Ezra was the first to speak. "I've been thinking that we need a plan to accomplish what we want to do this spring and summer."

"But we do have a plan," retorted Zeeney. "We are building a boat."

"Well, that's what's wrong," Ezra said. "You all arrive here every morning and start chiseling."

"Yeah, we are building the boat, that is the plan," Toby offered.

"That's the problem," said Ezra. "What are we going to do next and then after that? We need a plan, one on paper."

"All right, a plan, but since we have never built a boat before how are we even going to know how to plan one?" asked Zeeney.

Toby chimed in, " Why don't we take the drawing of the boat and break it down in sections. That way we can figure out which section needs to be built next."

"That's right," said Zeeney, "and we already have number one, number two, and number three. One, chop down tree, two, hollow out boat, and three steal blocks for rigging."

Zeeney was very proud; he had never planned anything before in his life.

Ezra, trying not to damper Zeeney's enthusiasm, said, "Well yes that is a good start, but we've already done those things, and I don't think we should write the word 'steal' in any of our plans, just in case they fall into the wrong hands."

Ezra started to write his list on parchment.

1. *Learn to swim.*
2. *Finish the interior of the boat.*
3. *Get the masts and booms.*
4. *Get the tent top and cut it into sails.*
5. *Finish the exterior of the boat.*
6. *Dig a trench for the boat next to the Creek.*
7. *Haul the boat from the rise to the Creek bed.*
8. *Tar the bottom of the boat.*
9. *Paint the boat.*
10. *Install the masts and booms including rigging.*
11. *Name the boat.*
12. *Flood the trench for the boat.*
13. *Haul the boat to the trench.*
14. *Check to make sure the boat does not leak.*
15. *Make the rudder, outriggers, and oars.*
16. *Christen and launch the boat.*

When he completed the list he read it to Toby and Zeeney, they could both read, but not very well.

"Number 1," Ezra started, "learn to swim."

"What!" Toby said. "What does that have to do with building a boat?"

Ezra explained, "We don't know for sure where our adventure will take us, or under what conditions. You two don't know how to swim, but I do. We will start each day for the next week by clearing the creek bed, then we'll cool off over there," Ezra pointed to the shallow area of the creek. "While we cool off, I'll teach the two of you how to swim. We will still do our other projects, but we will not complete number 16 until we are satisfied that you two swim well enough that if the boat sunk off shore, you could swim to shore and not drown."

After the list was read it was jointly decided that they would post the list inside the shed where only they could see it. They would then consult the list whenever necessary to make sure they kept to the schedule. It was now May 8th; they decided that July 8th, two months away would be their targeted completion date. They felt that all sixteen points could be completed easily in that time. Coincidentally, Ezra's thirteenth birthday also fell on July 8th. They would have two things to celebrate that day. They had a plan!

Since it was now mid-day they could not start any new projects. They would use the rest of that day to continue to chisel the interior and devote some time to creek bed clearing. They had to remove the debris pile from the boat to work on it, but kept it next to the boat just in case any outsiders happened by. They also knew that once the boat was hauled to the creek bed, they would have to conceal it until it was rigged. They would devise a means to conceal the boat in the trench once they got to that point. Once rigged, however, they had no idea how they would conceal the boat. They decided to cross that bridge when they arrived at that point. It was too far away to worry about that day.

After several days of working on the new plan it seemed to Zeeney that they were constantly running to the shed to consult the list. This would tell them what they were to do next but it was not a schedule, just a plan. For the next few evenings, he took it upon himself to create a schedule with actual dates of the start of each component on the list. He did not read very well, but decided that if he were to copy the list down word for word and reconstruct it at night, he would surely understand enough words in order to make a calendar of events.

He also decided that the calendar would be very short, starting on May 8th, and ending on July 8th. Since none of them had discussed any plans beyond July 8th, it would stop right there. All they knew beyond July 8th was that the sailing adventure would begin.

1746

	Sun	Mon	Tue	Wed	Thur	Fri	Sat
May	8	9	10	11	12	13	14
	The Plan	Start Interior					
	15	16	17	18	19	20	21
	Finish Interior	Masts		Tent Top	Start Exterior		
	22	23	24	25	26	27	28
				Finish Exterior		Start Trench	
	29	30	31				
June				1	2	3	4
				Haul			
				Finish	Boat	Tar	
				Trench	to Creek	Bottom	
	5	6	7	8	9	10	11
		Start to Paint				Hood Trench	
	12	13	14	15	16	17	18
	Haul Boat	to Trench		Start Rudder			
	19	20	21	22	23	24	25
	26	27	28	29	30		
		Rig Boat					
July						1	2
	3	4	5	6	7	8	
						Launch!	

Zeeney liked this much better. Instead of just a list with points to accomplish, he now had created a real schedule. He was not sure if they could keep to the schedule, but it allowed enough time between points to catch up if they fell behind. Also, instead of just checking off points from the list, they would know exactly what was coming next and when it should be completed. Yes, he liked it, he just hoped Toby and Ezra would feel the same way.

Chapter 14

When Ezra arrived the next morning, just as planned, Toby and Zeeney were clearing the creek bed.

"The plan is working, one day in a row!"

They decided together to work for three hours on the creek bed, and wait until the sun was a little higher in the morning sky before they would start their first swimming lesson. Ezra was as nervous as Toby and Zeeney. They had never swum before but Ezra had never taught anyone how to swim before either. As he worked on the creek bed, he thought of a plan. Ezra felt that the two boys were mostly afraid of water because they had never spent much time, if any, in or around it. Ezra, on the other hand, had been introduced to water as a young child and had learned how to swim at a very young age. He had respect but not fear of water. He thought that they would start in the shallows, just splashing and playing. The water would feel good after working in the dusty and warm creek bed. After a time, determined by the reactions of Toby and Zeeney, he would gradually coax them to slightly deeper water. The actual swimming lessons would probably not take place for several days. They should have fun first before they actually learned. Ezra also thought about the level the boys should reach before he would be satisfied. He really did not think they had to be proficient swimmers, but they should be able to breathe and float for an extended period of time above the water's surface without panicking. He thought, but did not know for sure, that it was panic, not lack of skill, that caused most novice swimmers to drown. Ezra felt that a modified breaststroke would be the best way for them to learn. First, though, they would play.

Ezra, Toby, and Zeeney left the creek bed. They took off their overalls, stripping down to their long johns. Ezra entered first. Toby and Zeeney looked a little cautious, but eventually, they walked a few feet into the water and pretended to splash and have fun. Ezra looked back and could tell that Toby and Zeeney were just not having fun. He saw a bucket sitting on shore that they used to fetch water while working. He ran over and grabbed the bucket. He filled it and threw the contents at Zeeney and he did the same to Toby. With each splash the boys started to laugh, just a little at first, then harder with each progressive dousing. The water felt really good after working in the dusty creek bed. Ezra could tell that this was working. He wanted them to associate water with fun, and swim lessons would come later. He really knew it was working when Toby and Zeeney rushed him between bucket filling, grabbed the bucket, wrestled Ezra to the shallow creek and doused him with the bucket. Now they were all having fun.

The three boys frolicked in the water for about two hours. They even ventured into deeper water, but not much more than just over waist deep. Ezra was pleased "Not bad for the first day," he thought.

As they left the water and walked ashore, they all knew it was time to work, but they had a problem. Their shore clothes were dry, but their woolen long johns were soaked through and would take a while to dry out. None of the boys had ever been naked in front of the others, and today was not going to be the first time. They would have to let the long johns dry on them, although that would probably take until the next day. That would be very uncomfortable at the least. They all determined that they would have to bring an extra pair of long johns to the creek bed to keep in the shed for swimming lessons. This way they could change into them every day and have dry long johns to change back into once the swim lessons were done. Today, they would have to tough it out and work with wet long johns. They had to keep on schedule and this afternoon was planned for sculpting the interior of the boat.

Every morning on previous days when Ezra arrived, Toby and Zeeney had always been working on the boat. Initially, the boys used rough axes to hollow out the interior. They had to be very careful not to remove more material from the boat than the intended finished size. Once again they realized that they did not really know what the finished size would be. Toby and Zeeney had worked each day with large chisels and hammers, carefully removing material. They discussed it and decided they had to make some exact measurements. They did not want the boat to be too thick or too thin any place within the interior or exterior. Ezra told Toby about the measuring stick he had designed to draw up the sails. He would bring that tomorrow and use it to design more measuring devices to aid in the final stages. They wanted to switch to the finer chisels, but were concerned that they might end up with a hole in the boat, or at the very least a weak spot that would fail at exactly the most inopportune time. They would suspend work for the day and start early the next morning. They were not disappointed about quitting early. Their scratchy wet long johns were really bothersome and they could not wait to get home and get them off. They would definitely bring an extra pair the next day to leave in the shed. They did not want to deal with this kind of misery again.

Chapter 15

It was Thursday, May 12th and work was going quite well. Everyone showed up with their extra long johns and Ezra brought his measuring stick. He added it to the other master measuring sticks and started making more at various lengths. They would use these to make sure their fine tune chiseling was accurate. They had not yet thought of how they would gauge the thickness of the hull, but thought they would determine that when it was time to start on the exterior. So, each day they would chisel, clear the creek bed, and swim. Not a bad way to spend a spring.

By May 15th the interior was complete, right on schedule. The boys were incredibly excited, they knew the masts and booms were complete and that they were a day ahead of schedule. They decided that even though they were ahead of schedule, they could not wait to bring the mast and booms to the creek bed. They would wait however. They still needed to come up with a thickness gauge to aid them in finishing the exterior. The very bottom would be easy because they could use the measuring sticks that they had created to measure from the ground to the bottom of the inverted boat. They already knew the distance from the boat's rail to the bottom by sliding a very straight board down the boat from bow to stern and placing a measuring stick secured by leather strapping to this board. They were careful not to remove more material than the length of this stick. Luckily the stick always hit something and they would slowly chisel until the stick barely touched. This was a tedious, but necessary process. They decided it was now time to invert the boat. The bulk of the wood had been removed and they could roll it over, but they would still need the plow horse to get the boat to the creek bed. Even though the boat was still on the incline of the rise, they could work with it. They transferred the measurements from the rail to the bottom of the boat. They decided that the finished thickness of the bottom of the boat would be 1-1/4" greater than the length from the rail to the interior floor. They really did not know why 1-1/4" seemed appropriate, but anything thicker seemed too thick and would just add weight to the boat. Anything any thinner might detrimentally affect the integrity of the boat. They were not going into the ocean, but they wanted a craft that was safe in the bay storms that often came from nowhere. Next, they had to gauge the exterior thickness.

Zeeney was playing with different ideas. He knew he could use only the implements he had on hand as he did not want Ezra to organize another "shopping trip." In looking at some of the measuring sticks, he thought that if he could secure them side by side with leather straps and tie them apart with some sort of spacer, he could create a gap between the two long sticks of 1-1/4". He would then have a device to measure the thickness of the side of the boat. It had to be long enough to fit from the rail to the bottom and it could not flex. What he finally came up with were two very long measuring sticks, strapped side by side. He strapped two similar sticks the same way. He laid the two sets of strapped sticks parallel to each other 3-1/4" apart. He then took six small flat boards he had found in the shed and strapped four at the end of the new tool. He noticed that at the unstrapped, or measuring end, there was too much flex between the two sets of sticks. He measured from the end to find the distance from the top rail to the bottom of the boat, about 18". At this point, he tied off the two remaining sticks. This gave the tool the rigidity it would need and it would easily reach down the side of the boat, but not to the very curvature that connected the bottom to the sides. He chose a gap between the sets of sticks of 3-1/4", because this would allow him to strap two 1" iron cleats, one on each side, at the very end of the device, creating a very rigid gauge exactly 1-1/4" wide. He could now easily hold the tool with the three boards at the top, with the two sticks in the middle adding rigidity to the two parallel sticks. The device would work. They could measure as far down the sides as they pleased to gauge the final thickness of the boat. Zeeney knew that since they already knew the depth of the boat from rail to interior bottom, that they could use that measurement, adding 1-1/4" to it, when they inverted the boat and started to sculpt the exterior bottom. He was confident that the bottom, as well as the sides, would be exact, and he felt equally confident that the curvature from the bottom to the sides could be easily chiseled by just sighting down the length of the boat. They were ready to retrieve the masts and booms that were a major milestone in their boat building process.

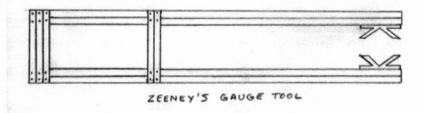

ZEENEY'S GAUGE TOOL

Chapter 16

The morning of May 16th, Ezra awoke with a big smile. The masts and booms were ready, and he could not wait to see them. After a quick breakfast, he ran to Elizabeth's house. He felt it was the right thing to do given the fact that Elizabeth had made all the arrangements and he did not know Elizabeth's grandfather all that well. He suggested that Toby and Zeeney meet him at the woodworking shop around nine thirty, neither of the two boys could tell time, therefore they would have to ask someone when nine-thirty was. They usually started much earlier each day but that day, being very special, they wanted to make sure nothing was rushed. Ezra knocked on Elizabeth's door. She was expecting him and answered the door with a huge smile.

"Good morning," said Ezra.

"Good morning!" gushed Elizabeth.

She was so excited to see Ezra. He was so excited to finally get his masts and booms.

"I saw grandfather yesterday. The tent poles should be done this morning. They look very beautiful. Grandfather did an especially good job because they are for your mother. He truly likes your mother."

Ezra did not hear a word Elizabeth was saying. He just stared at her with a grin, picturing in his mind how the masts and booms would look on the unnamed boat. Elizabeth saw Ezra's grin and thought, "He must like me after all."

Ezra and Elizabeth headed down the narrow dirt path that linked Elizabeth's house to the woodwork shop. Elizabeth's entire family worked there, her father, her mother, and her two older brothers. Elizabeth herself was too young to work there or any place on the plantation. She went to school daily, but could go to work, as Ezra assumed he would, when she turned thirteen. All the way down the path, Elizabeth talked about the upcoming summer and all the fun they would have at the beach.

"What a wonderful idea the beach tent is!" she said. "Would it be alright for my family to use it when Mrs. Pooles isn't there?"

Ezra was paying no attention whatsoever to what Elizabeth was saying.

"We'll erect the masts, attach the booms, and then start on the rigging," he thought. "Then she'll look like a real boat!"

"She," he thought. It was the first time he had referred to the yet unnamed boat as anything other than "the boat." He knew it was common practice to refer to boats as "she," and not "he." He had not thought of "the boat" as either gender, but would do so from that point on. He also thought they had better start to think of a name for "her."

When they arrived at Elizabeth's grandfather's woodworking shop, Toby and Zeeney were already there.

"Good morning Miss Elizabeth," they said in unison, rising to greet Ezra and Elizabeth.

"Good morning boys," replied Elizabeth. " I'll go inside to see if grandfather has completed your tent poles." She entered leaving the three anxious boys to wait.

Toby said to Ezra, "I was thinking we probably should paint the poles once we get them. What do you think Zeeney?"

"Yes, we probably should."

Just then, Elizabeth popped her head through the entrance of the woodworking shop. She was beaming.

"They are ready and they are beautiful. Please come inside."

When they entered the shop they were surprised at the size of it. This shop created all of the wooden implements that where used on the plantation. Additionally, since they had the capacity, skill, and craftsmanship, they also produced high quality wooden pieces. The shop also included a clockmaking shop to produce tall case clocks. Only two or three of these, Ezra soon found out, were manufactured each year. All of the pieces to the clocks were prefabricated in the shop. The clock works were imported from Bavaria. Ezra knew that the woodworking shop was an ambitious undertaking, but he no idea that many of the items that they made were destined to be sold in Baltimore and Philadelphia, and in some rare cases, New York. Elizabeth's grandfather's shop was renowned for its quality and always had back-orders for the different wooden treasures they produced.

Elizabeth's grandfather approached the diminutive group wiping his hands with a rag as he approached.

"Good morning boys and Elizabeth," he said. "My name is Samuel Thomas. Welcome to my shop! I understand you are here to retrieve the tent poles that we made for you. Quite unusual, those poles, some real tall, and some real short. For a tent I understand?"

"Yes sir," Ezra chimed in. "They are a surprise birthday present for my mother."

"Yes, I understood that," replied Samuel. "We did them free of charge because they are for Mrs. Pooles. I always liked her, kind lady."

Ezra never thought that there could be a charge associated with anything on the plantation. He had never purchased anything in his life. In fact, he had never possessed money, therefore a charge for the "tent poles" never entered his mind. "Guess I got lucky again," he thought.

"Walk this way. Your poles are in the finishing room," Mr. Thomas said.

The group slowly made there way through the bustle of activity. Since Toby and Zeeney had never worked there and Ezra had never worked at all, the different tools and machines they passed fascinated them. There were saws, lathes, and grinding devices of every imaginable size and shape. The boys could not even query the function of most of these. To Elizabeth, it was old hat, even boring. All of these "machines" were connected to leather belts that entered the building through the floor at the location of each machine. Mr. Thomas explained over the din that the leather belt was used to run all the machines, that each machine had a lever that allowed the workers to engage the machine to the continuously running belt. He further explained that this belt was connected to a large water wheel located outside the building and driven by a small stream that ran past the woodworking shop on its way to the Patapsco River. Sawdust was everywhere and the boys loved the smell; they were reminded of the smell of working on the boat. They walked into another area separated by large doors. In this room were large stacks of yet uncut logs stacked according to their type. They walked through another set of doors with finished wooden planks that had been roughly cut to reveal the best part of the trees, most were clear cuts with no knots. Through yet another set of large doors, there was a storeroom full of finished goods. This was obviously the room where items were prepared for shipping, not only to the plantation, but also far away places. The boys noticed that Samuel was very careful to close each set of doors as they entered a room and before he would open the next set. They wondered why he did not just leave the doors open if they were coming back this way with the long poles.

When they entered the last room, they received the answer to their question. Samuel was giving a mini- tour as they walked, with basic explanations of the functions of many of the machines. He also explained how work moved through the shop and the function of each of the rooms they had passed.

When they entered the next room he asked, "What do you think is the biggest problem we have at the shop?"

"Finding wood?" asked Toby,

"No, finding customers," replied Zeeney.

"I bet it's coming up with the designs," added Ezra.

Elizabeth could barely hold back the real answer and had a smirk on her face.

"Sawdust!" Samuel spouted out. "Sawdust! We make so much when we tool the wood, and as you could see in the previous rooms, it's everywhere. We have these large rooms separated by swinging doors to try to keep the sawdust out. That is why I am careful to close one set before opening the next. It is also why this last room, the finishing room, is a far as possible from the cutting room. No matter how careful we are, we can't avoid the sawdust. I guess if the finishing room were in another building, or better yet, another county, we might avoid the mess it makes. Sawdust sure makes it hard to finish." He stopped, looked around the room, "Your tent poles are in that corner," he said, as he pointed toward the back corner of the very large room with its very high ceiling.

The boys moved very quickly in the direction that Samuel had indicated. Surprisingly at first they did not see the poles because there were so many items in the finishing room. When they finally found the poles, they were laid out on the ground suspended a few inches above the pine planked floor. Each pole sat on some type of cloth that separated them from the rough wooden supports that sat beneath them. The boys stopped. They all opened their mouths, but no words came out. They were all unusually speechless. Ezra was the first to speak.

"They are beautiful, Mr. Thomas," he said.

They were not only one-third of their original size, they were uniform and tapered. Surprisingly, and more importantly, each "tent pole" had been painstakingly finished. Obviously they were smoothed, but also stained and varnished. They were a real piece of art.

"Yes," Samuel interjected, "I decided to make those tent poles real pretty for your mother. She won't get any splinters touching these poles. Don't quite understand your design, Son. Why are some so tall and some so short?" questioned Samuel.

Ezra had anticipated this question and already devised an answer.

"Well it gets real windy on the beach in the summer, especially when storms come up. I didn't want the tent to get blown away, so I decided to make them extra long to bury the real tall ones deep in the sand. This will give the tent stability when the wind gusts. The shorter ones will just sit directly on the ground. I thought it would be a good idea to make the tent different levels to make the hot summer air flow inside the tent."

Samuel looked down at the "tent poles," scratched his head and said, "Shame to bury so much of those pretty poles in the sand, but I guess you know what you are doing Son."

Toby and Zeeney started to pick up the heavy poles. They asked Mr. Samuel if they could have the pieces of cloth to separate the poles.

"No problem," replied Samuel.

The two boys picked up the longer two poles while Ezra grabbed the shorter two, one in each hand. As they carefully lifted the poles, they all admired how beautiful they were. The grain of the oak was gorgeous and the stain and varnish enhanced the beauty even more.

"Sure is a shame to cover up this beautiful wood with sailcloth," Zeeney thought.

They slowly wound their way through the finishing shop. It was particularly hard for Toby and Zeeney to maneuver the long poles, and not much easier for Ezra because he had two poles of different lengths to deal with. The last thing any of them wanted to do was to strike something on the way out. This would possibly damage the poles or other items in the finishing room. They knew Samuel would not be happy either way. They walked slowly and carefully.

"Your mother is really going to be happy with this tent," Elizabeth blurted out.

"Yes," Ezra replied, "very happy."

Chapter 17

The boys just kept looking down at the beautiful new tools for the boat. Now they couldn't wait for the day they would actually install them. For the first time, they all felt that it was actually going to happen, they were going to launch and sail this boat. They decided that the best path to the creek bed was not the direct route through the plantation, but the longer way down to the water and along the creek road. This was the same dirt road his father had used several days earlier to check on Ezra. This way was probably twice as long, but they knew that it was a very isolated road only traveled by anyone wishing to go to the creek bed. Ezra did not know why the road existed because until the "boat-yard" was completed, there was no reason for anyone to use it.

He wondered about the road briefly, but then thought more about why they would use this much longer route. The more direct trek through the plantation would certainly save time, but it would also bring them in contact with more people than was prudent. They were positive that anyone they encountered would be curious about the long poles they carried and would surely inquire as to their intended use. The fewer people that knew about the existence of the "masts/booms/tent poles," the better. So, they headed west toward the water, and once they arrived there, off down the narrow dirt road they went. As they walked, all of the boys had to take breaks, the poles were fairly heavy, so from time to time they carefully laid them down in the grass that lined the dirt road. None of the boys had ever spent any time on this part of the land. Ezra commented that it is actually quite beautiful. The narrow dirt road ran along the waters edge. In fact, at high tide and when the wind was blowing strongly from the west, some flooding would take place along the shoreline. But not that day, that day the water gently lapped the shoreline that bordered the dirt road. On the landside of the road were tall pines, below the pines was thick underbrush that offered limited visibility into the woods. It was a beautiful sunny day and not terribly breezy.

Toby asked Ezra, "Will we sail by here when we start exploring?"

Ezra replied, "I think so, but I think too that it will depend on the direction of the wind."

This was really the first time any of them had paid any attention to wind direction, or for that matter, wind at all.

They finally made the last turn at the tree line, the place where Toby and Zeeney had seen the last horse disappear the day that Mr. Pooles had come to visit. The creek bed was in sight and their long journey nearly complete.

"The next time we use these," Zeeney explained, speaking of the masts and booms, "instead of us carrying them, they'll be carrying us." An instant mental picture of the sailing boat entered their minds, for the first time they could all visualize it on the water and under sail.

They walked through the creek bed and started up the rise. The poles were easy to carry now. They only had to maneuver the short distance up the rise, and past the boat and felled tree to the shed. Ezra already knew that the poles would not fit in the small shed. Either laying down or standing up, they were simply too long. The shorter two actually would fit, but there was no sense in storing two in and two out. If they weathered, they should all weather the same, he thought. The plan was to find as flat an area as possible to lay them side-by-side. They would hide them with more fern fronds that would both conceal and protect them from weather.

Behind the shed and a little further up the rise was a natural ledge that was perfect. With a little work they could easily conceal the poles with the fronds. The boys thought that once the fronds turn brown, it may appear that they were placed there by nature deterring any outsiders from picking them to discover what was beneath. They also decided that this was the last day that they would be known as tent poles. The next time they touched them would be as the forward and aft rig of the boat.

Chapter 18

T he next day, May 18th, was another routine day for the boys. They cleared the creek bed all morning, and then swam for about two hours. Their swim was far more pleasant this day because they were wearing their swimming long johns. Knowing that they had dry clothes to change into at the shed made an enormous difference. Zeeney suggested that the next day they cut the legs and arms of the long johns shorter for an even better experience. They ventured into even deeper water, this day up to their chests, but they were still in the playing stage, Ezra did not want to rush the process and they still had a lot of time before the launch date.

This day was also the first day that they were to work on the exterior bottom. The interior was almost complete, they just had to do some minor finishing and bore holes to insert the two masts. Installing the masts was in the schedule Zeeney had created for sometime late in June. Before inverting the boat by simply rolling it over, the boys double-checked their measurements from the rail to the interior bottom. They did this by laying a very straight stick to straddle the two rails and then measured from the interior bottom of the boat to the bottom of the stick. When the boat was inverted and as they started to carefully hack the bottom away, they would periodically check their progress with three sticks that they joined into a square with the top missing. From the end of each of the two parallel sticks to the adjoined stick at the top, it was exactly 1-1/4" greater than the distance they had measured from the rails to the interior bottom. From time to time they would stop the hacking and one boy on one side of the boat would align the end of the stick with the rail. If the other boy on the other side could not reach the rail, it indicated how much more material they would have to remove. The third boy, at the bow, would sight down the length of the boat to make sure that the bottom was parallel to the two rails. This was very tedious, but necessary work. They could leave slightly more material on the bottom that would be removed with chisels, but if they removed too much they had no way to add the material back. If that happened their project would come to an abrupt end. Knowing this, all three boys were very careful and took great care to measure frequently.

When the boys had taken Mr. Thomas' tour of the woodworking shop, one of the tools that impressed them was a scraping tool. This was a long steel bar that had a tiny curved tip at the end. The workers in the cutting room would use these bars to do the final finish to the piece they were working on. They were shown various bars in different lengths and thicknesses. Mr. Thomas also showed the boys that the bars had different sizes and shapes of curves at their ends. These differences would determine how much material they would remove with a single pull; they would use the widest bars, with the smallest curves at the very end of the job to produce the smoothest results. Ezra thought about these tools and how he would go about obtaining them before the boat was complete. He wanted the boat to be as perfect as possible. The boys knew they were eventually going to paint the boat and paint would only accentuate an uneven surface.

It was Ezra's job to stand at the bow and sight down the bottom while Toby and Zeeney handled the measuring sticks and did the hacking. The three boys had determined early on that, for some reason, Ezra had a better sense of spatial symmetry.

He would observe from the bow and give the order to stop and measure. Occasionally, he would wander to the stern of the boat to examine the progress from that perspective.

Wednesday, May 19th, was another milestone day. Finally, they were to go to the seamstress shop to pick up the tent top that they would later cut into sails. They decided to take a little break in their routine and not go to the creek bed that morning. They could not pick up the tent top until early afternoon, so they decided they would just stay around their homes until the time arrived. They were to meet at the seamstress shop at one- thirty. Again Toby and Zeeney would have to consult the people who worked around their homes to be made aware of the time. At about one-fifteen they left, they knew it was ten-minute walk, but did not want to wait. At exactly one-thirty, Ezra arrived. As usual, Toby and Zeeney were already there.

Miss Lucy was the head seamstress. When she received the unusual request along with the specific drawing that accompanied it, she had doubts. She knew she would have to consult someone on this matter. When she questioned Elizabeth she was told that it was a special surprise and had to be kept a secret. Elizabeth also told Miss Lucy that her grandfather was involved and was already making the tent poles that would be accompanying the tent top. Miss Lucy thought it would be prudent to talk to Mr. Thomas before proceeding. That afternoon, during her scheduled break, she took the time to see Mr. Thomas. She carried with her the coal drawing that Elizabeth had given her. When she arrived at the woodworking shop, Mr. Thomas was also taking his afternoon break. This was lucky for Miss Lucy. She did not like the noise of the place and feared that her long skirts would become entangled in the exposed leather belts. The place made her very nervous.

"Good afternoon," stated Miss Lucy.

"Good afternoon to you as well," Mr. Thomas replied. "To what pleasure may I attribute this visit?"

"Well," Miss Lucy responded, "it's about this."

She hand the drawing of the tent top to Mr. Thomas. It was quite smeared now, but still legible? Mr. Thomas adjusted his glasses and examined the rough drawing

"Your granddaughter gave this to me. It's supposed to be a surprise for Miss Emily, it's to be the top of a tent."

Mr. Thomas stopped examining the strange drawing and dropped it to his side. He then handed it back to Miss Lucy.

"Yes, I know all about it. In fact, we just finished constructing the tent poles. I must say it is the most unusual tent I have ever seen. The tent poles are very unusual lengths, but Miss Emily's son, Ezra, gave it to Elizabeth and asked that they be constructed in secrecy, for her birthday I'm told."

Miss Lucy still looked perplexed as she received the drawing back from Mr. Thomas.

"But who's going to pay for this?" she asked.

"I thought about this when Elizabeth first approached me." Mr. Thomas answered.

"Normally I would go to Mr. Pooles and get his approval, but Elizabeth insisted that this was a surprise and no one, especially Mr. Pooles, could know about it. Otherwise, he would surely mention it to Mrs. Pooles and the surprise would be over. What I did was to add the cost to the general plantation ledger, and broke the cost down as several unrelated items. At first my inclination was to make them for free, but after more thought, I had no way to cover the cost of the material and labor. I have not informed the boy yet, but will the next time I see him. I'm sure that Mr. Pooles will question those charges, but he doesn't audit the ledger until the end of summer. By then, Mrs. Pooles will have her surprise and the charges will be easy to explain. I would suggest that you do the same."

Miss Lucy thanked Mr. Thomas for his suggestions. She would do the same. Since she now knew she could proceed, she wondered what she would use to make the tent top. When Elizabeth had made her request and given her the drawing, she had asked that the tent top be light, but strong, and it would help if the material was water resistant.

As Miss Lucy hurried back to the seamstress shop she wondered, "What material do we have enough of that would work for this job?"

She thought for a while then remembered some material that was in the loft. It had been there for quite a while. Mr. Pooles had ordered it years ago from a shop in Baltimore town, but for some reason never used the material to make anything. It would probably work, there was enough of it, it was fairly light and strong, but she did not know if it was water resistant. Then she thought, "Well, I can't think of everything, if it's water resistant, that's a bonus. If not, then too damn bad. I don't like to take special requests like this, especially this special! Yes, that material will just have to do."

Then she thought about the material some more. What kind of material was it? Then she remembered that it was called 'sailcloth.'

"Maybe 'sailcloth' will make a good tent top," she thought as she entered the seamstress shop.

Chapter 19

The tent top was neatly folded in the corner. The ladies that worked there had to drag the top out into the field to fold it. They were careful to walk around the field to find a clear area to lay it out; they had worked hard and long on it. The tent top was not complicated and the drawing was clear enough to follow, but the size and weight of the tent top made the work laborious. When it was finally complete, Miss Lucy knew that they could not fold it properly in the confines of the shop. They wanted to fold it neatly and store it in the corner where it would be picked up, she assumed, by Ezra Pooles. After all, Elizabeth had told her that Ezra Pooles had requested the tent top and created the drawing.

It took ten of the seamstresses that worked in the shop to carry the top outside. Once they found a clear spot, one that was clear of horse or other animal waste, they dropped the tent top and spread it out. In carrying it they bunched the material together as best they could to keep it from dragging on the floor and possibly snagging on a nail and tearing. Once on the field it was fairly easy to spread out. They took turns carrying the corners of the top to the other corners, they did this until the top was a fairly small, but neat bundle. Getting the top from the field back into the shop was harder than they had anticipated. Although they were ten fairly strong women, the folded top was now bulky and heavy, and there was no place to hold on to it. The best they could do was to carry the folded top several feet before they would sit it back on the ground. After each attempt they would have to regain their strength before trying again. It took a good four times longer to get the top back in as to carry it out. When they finally dropped the top in the corner, they knew they were done with it, and they were very relieved. Whoever picked up this heavy top was on their own, but all of the ladies, including Miss Lucy would be very happy to see it disappear out the door.

Ezra, as usual, arrived several minutes after Toby and Zeeney. They approached the seamstress shop and asked for Miss Lucy. Ezra had been told by Elizabeth that Miss Lucy was preparing the top and that she would be the one to contact when it was ready. They asked the first lady, who was busy sewing, where they could find Miss Lucy. Without looking up she pointed in Miss Lucy's direction. The boys approached Miss Lucy, removed their hats, Ezra introduced himself and the boys.

"Miss Lucy, I'm Ezra Pooles, these here boys are Toby and Zeeney. We are here to pick up to tent top you so kindly made for my mother."

Miss Lucy looked up at the boys and nodded to Ezra's introduction. She looked at Ezra, then Toby, then Zeeney. She then looked around the back of where the boys stood confused, they looked back as well. "Where's your help?" Miss Lucy asked.

Ezra, still looking confused said, "Oh, we don't need help. We can handle it just fine."

At that the other ladies in the room started to giggle.

"So you three strong boys are going to lift that top over in the corner and carry it out of here?"

"Yes ma'am," Ezra replied.

The ladies' giggles broke into laughter.

Miss Lucy, in a very stern voice, said loudly, "Ladies, I don't know what is so funny. Get back to work." With that statement, instead of silencing the ladies, they laughed even harder and louder. Miss Lucy's stern look crumbled as she started laughing as well. "It's over in that corner," she pointed through her laughter. "Good luck."

Ezra, Toby, and Zeeney were puzzled.

"These ladies sure do enjoy their work," Toby said.

The boys proceeded toward the tent top that was in the corner. Ezra went to one side, Toby and Zeeney to the other two exposed sides. They each reached down and slid their hands under the top.

"Alright lift," Ezra ordered. They attempted, but only grunts came from the boys; the heavy top did not budge. The now silent seamstresses stopped their work to watch the boys. They all smiled but as soon as they heard the grunt and the top did not budge, they again burst into laughter, even Miss Lucy. The boys tried again, and again nothing but a grunt. The boys were starting to understand what was so funny! Them!

Four more failed attempts were made by the boys, as the laughter continued. After the fourth try it was obvious that the heavy top was not going to simply walk out of the seamstress shop. Even if it did, how could they possibly transport it all the way to the creek bed? They would have to take a similar route along the dirt road by the river, but how could they possibly accomplish this? It was obvious to the boys that despite their well thought out plans, they had not anticipated this problem. They would leave the seamstress shop and go somewhere quiet to come up with a plan. There had to be a way.

Chapter 20

Life was certainly easier for the boys now that Mr. Pooles had made the creek bed a legitimate job. No longer would they have to plot anymore raids like the one they had carried out at Old Mr. Jim's. They were still stinging from the previous day's encounter at the seamstress shop. When they realized that the ladies were laughing at them, it hurt their feelings. After all, they were fearless adventurers; they couldn't have a bunch of ladies making fun of them. They decided that the best course of action when they returned to the seamstress shop to fetch their sails was to be prepared and really know what they were doing. They could not tolerate any more laughter, especially from a bunch of women.

They could now easily get any implement they required. All they had to say is that it was for the creek bed job that Mr. Pooles had ordered. If anyone should contact Mr. Pooles to verify their requests, he would surely say that he had authorized the boys to do this work and anything they needed to complete the job could be obtained. Yes, life was certainly going to be easier.

They knew they needed several things to get the sails to the creek bed. Now that the tent top was completed, they no longer referred to it as a tent top, but as the sails they needed. They only referred to them as sails among themselves, however to everyone else it was still a tent top. They knew they would need a horse and cart; they would also need several men to help carry the sail from the seamstress shop to the cart. Once at the creek bed, the boys felt that they could at least push the heavy sails from the cart onto the ground. Spreading the sails on the creek bed should be simple. They did not want the men needed to carry the sails to the cart at the creek bed. Although they covered the boat each day as they finished their work, they did not want to take the chance of any curious men seeing something they shouldn't. Even a mention to Mr. Pooles might cause him to visit again to investigate.

As they talked they thought of other items that would be needed and were easily covered by the authority Mr. Pooles had given them. The horse and cart were easy. The men would be a little more difficult, but if they got them early enough in the morning no one would question their plea for help. The men could meet them at the seamstress shop before they started their days work. While at the seamstress shop they would also ask Miss Lucy to borrow some shears, needles, thread, and any other implements they would need to complete the modifications to the sails. They were aware that Miss Lucy might ask why they needed them and there answer would be simple. Modifications would be necessary as the tent was erected. As the boys did not know for sure what those modifications might be, they wanted the tools at their site when, and if, they were needed. Any items borrowed would be returned as soon as the tent was erected. This gave them more time than necessary to keep these items. The boys discussed the fact that none of them had ever sewn anything in their lives, but they all came to the same conclusion.

"How hard can it be if a bunch of women do it?"

In addition to the items that they already knew they needed, they also decided to combine this job with a side trip to the woodworking shop. There they would ask Mr. Thomas to borrow, under Mr. Pooles' authority, several of the steel bar scrapers that they had seen there

Ezra was elated. "Yes sir, the wide one there, 3" with the fine curve. It will be perfect." Ezra pointed to the instrument of his desire.

"Fine son," said Mr. Thomas. "You fetch the one you want, and sign my ledger before you go. I want to make sure that this is acceptable with your father."

Ezra had not thought of this. If Mr. Thomas went to his father with this terribly expensive charge, he had no idea how father would react. His only hope was that Mr Thomas would forget to ask Father and Father would not see the charge until the end of the summer audit. He was already in deep. For some reason, he thought the tent poles and top were all free; he now was aware that all of these charges were on the ledger and would suffer Mr. Pooles' examination later in the year. Ezra's goose was very well cooked already.

He gleefully chose the scraping implement that would finish the boat. As he walked to the horse cart, scraper in hand, he admired it and tried to put out of his thoughts what he had just done.

"Seventy-five pounds is a lot of money. I'm sure I will be in deep water once Father finds out, but I'll deal with that when the time comes."

Little did Ezra know that the total charges to date were not seventy-five pounds, but over two hundred-fifty pounds, an enormous sum that would definitely get his father's notice.

Chapter 21

Having the horse cart was certainly a better way to travel and the boys knew there was no way the sails would get there without it. The time it took was nothing compared to the day they carried the poles. Once at the creek bed, after they determined that the flat area of the creek bed was clean enough and free of obstructions that might damage their new sails, they pushed the heavy bundle from the cart to the creek bed. It took all three boys pushing as hard as they could, but it was easier than trying to lift it at the seamstress shop the day before. After the sail bundle hit the creek bed, they moved the horse cart down to the creek so that the horse could end his thirst and to allow room to spread out their new sail. It did not take them very long to lay out the sails on the creek bed. All three boys were surprised of the large size of the sails, but Ezra reminded them that they would be smaller and more manageable once they were cut into individual sails. The plan was to cut the two sails away and carefully trim away the waste area. Once this was done they would start to sew the cut edges to make the sails more presentable. They would also join the two remaining scrap pieces into a simple tent.

Ezra started at one end while Toby was at the other, both cutting with the shears that Miss Lucy had lent them. They were on the ledger as well. They took their time attempting to evenly divide the sacrificial strip that joined the two sails at their greatest length. They then headed to the opposite sides of the triangles to cut away the areas that were to become their tent for the trip. After cutting the last part, two nearly finished sails laid beneath them on the creek bed. They could not conceal their excitement! They would start sewing and sew for the rest of the day hoping to complete the sails at the very least. Whatever they were to do to the tent would come later.

As they worked silently, Zeeney finally exclaimed, "Ladies do this work?"

Sewing the sailcloth was far more difficult then they had imagined. The boys had to use pieces of flat boards to force the large needles through the sailcloth; it was definitely more difficult than any of the boys had thought, but by the end of that day they had their finished sails. They carefully folded first the sails and then the tent and carried them along with the scraper to the shed. Their new practice was to lock the shed each night as their valuable items started to accumulate. It had been a long, but very successful day. All three boys agreed they needed rest.

They returned the horse cart to the barn and bid each other good night as Ezra headed in one direction, Toby and Zeeney the other. They would meet early the next morning at the creek bed. The next day promised to be far more routine, clearing, swimming, and chiseling. They looked forward to it.

Chapter 22

The next day, the 21st of May, a Saturday, arrived. As usual Ezra arrived at the creek bed after Toby and Zeeney, but as soon as Ezra walked through the wooded area to the creek bed he knew something was terribly wrong. Instead of seeing the boy's backsides hunched over the boat working, they were tied back to back sitting in the middle of the creek bed. Both boys stared in Ezra's direction, tears streaming down their cheeks. Ezra looked in the direction of the boat as his father's men were hacking it to pieces with heavy axes. Between Ezra and the boat stood his father. At first he was a blur as Ezra could only focus on the destruction of his dream. Now clearly visible, Ezra could see the stern almost menacing look on his father's face.

"Ezra, come here now, you are in deep trouble!"

Ezra woke with a start.

It was a dream, or rather the worst nightmare that Ezra could imagine. He sat up in bed, breathing heavily and sweating profusely. As he slowly calmed down he wondered, "Was it a nightmare or simply a premonition of events to happen?"

He had to get to the creek bed. He dressed quickly, bypassing the breakfast he usually had before starting the day. As he nervously made his way through the wooded area just east of the creek bed, he expected the worst.

"It was a premonition," he thought. As he cleared out of the woods and could now clearly see the creek bed, Toby and Zeeney were nowhere to be seen. As Ezra scanned the horizon and made his glance direct toward the boat, instead of men hacking with axes, he observed Toby and Zeeney's backsides as they chiseled away at the bottom of the boat. Filled with relief, Ezra slowly made his way to the boat. As Ezra walked to the boat, he decided not to share his nightmare with the boys as he felt it would only worry them. They were both very superstitious and the thought of what had occurred in Ezra's dreams would probably haunt them every day from that day forward.

Ezra greeted the boys. They both turned and greeted Ezra with their usual smiles.

"Good morning," Ezra said to the boys, I was thinking on my way here this morning that we are way ahead of schedule, things are going very well. Why don't we take a break from the boat and work on the creek bed. I would like to start burning the large piles of debris that have accumulated there."

Toby and Zeeney both sighed as the smiles left their faces.

"While the piles are burning, we can observe them from the water while we swim."

The smiles returned.

The boys started to drag the piles of debris to the creek shoreline. They made sure to get the oldest piles first because they would be easier to burn. Ezra went to the shed to fetch the flints. While there he also changed into his swimming long johns. He could not help to noticing that they reeked. It was probably well past the time when they were washed with soap to eliminate the strong odor. He would discuss this with the boys who he was sure had noticed the odor as well. While he started the fires, he would send first one boy and then the other to change at the shed. That way at least two of the boys could watch the fires as the other one changed. Luckily, that day the wind was out of the southeast, so there was not a great concern about sparks being blown into the woods. It had been a very dry spring so far and the danger of a brush fire was extremely possible. Ezra recalled his father's warnings of burning the debris on the rise. As they romped in the water, they made certain to keep a watchful eye on the small fires burning on the shoreline.

The swimming lessons had proceeded very well. Ezra's plan for the boys to have fun had worked, but he knew that soon they would have to get down to the serious business of learning to swim. Each day before they had ventured farther and farther into the creek, but other than Toby's experience in the well, neither boy had been in water deep enough that they could not touch the bottom. Ezra brought them as far as they could go where they could still stand and their heads would be above the surface.

"So far, so good," Ezra thought, "but what next?" He could tell that both boys were getting nervous.

"I don't want you to leave where you are. I want you to still be able to touch the bottom but I am going to show you the swim stroke first, followed by the kick you will need to keep you afloat. Where I am, I cannot touch bottom," Ezra said to the boys. Ezra moved in circles using a modified breaststroke.

" I move my arms in front of me," he demonstrated, "moving them from the front to my sides. This propels my body and at the same time keeps me afloat. Also, at the same time, I am kicking my legs back and forth, which also acts to propel and keep me afloat. Where you stand now, I want you to practice the stroke first. Once you are comfortable with that try kicking. Stay where you can touch the bottom in case you get nervous, but try the stroke and the kick without touching to see if it works."

Both boys nervously did the breaststroke first and then the kick. At first their heads would slip below the surface and they would sputter gasping for air. Eventually they got the hang of it, swimming in circles, but never leaving the safety of the area where they could touch bottom if necessary. At this point, they were swimming; deeper water could come on another day. They had made enormous progress.

As they left the water and walked back to the shoreline, Ezra commented on the odor of long johns.

"I think we ought to wash these things before we swim again, they reek."

Both boys nodded in agreement, but Ezra knew what they were thinking. They could swim!

Chapter 23

Since they were well ahead of schedule, they decided jointly to take Sunday off. They really had not taken a break in some time and needed a rest from their routine, so what better day than Sunday to do just that. They would spend the day with their families, eat lots of food, take a nap or two; they might even squeeze in church. Come Monday they were back at it. According to Zeeney's schedule, Thursday was the day that they were to start digging the trench. That gave them three days to finish the exterior and bring the plow horse back to the creek bed to haul the boat to the creek bed. They knew that they wanted to take their time when they used the expensive scraping tool that they, or rather Mr. Pooles, had purchased from Mr. Thomas. They decided that it would be best to use the scraping tool after the horse dragged the boat from the rise to the creek bed near where the new trench was to be dug. If any damage occurred to the bottom while moving the boat, they could easily repair it with the scraping tool.

Their days were very easy now, with plenty of time to chisel and swim. On Tuesday they borrowed the plow horse again and headed to the creek bed. Zeeney rode while Toby and Ezra walked along side. As they walked they discussed their plan of action. They would nail two of the largest cleats on the rails nearest the bow, opposite of each other, and about a foot from the tip of the bow. They would use the longest, largest nails that they could find in the shed. They would mark the holes that would secure the cleats, and use the fine boring tools they found in the shed to pre-bore the nail holes. They did not want the rails to split as they introduced the nails. That would be disastrous!

When they arrived at the creek bed, Toby ran to the shed to start bringing the implements they would need. He selected the two largest cleats from their supply and he found the largest nails that would fit through the two holes in each cleat. He decided to bring extra nails, just in case. Then, he matched the nails to the boring tools to find one just slightly smaller than the nails. He grabbed everything, including a hammer, and lastly, grabbed a length of rope. He believed that he had everything they would need to do the job. He arrived back at the boat with all the tools and the three boys went to work.

First, they used the measuring stick to determine where to place the cleats, then to mark the cleat holes, to bore the holes, and finally to drive the large nails with the hammer to secure the cleats. The entire process took very little time. Next they were ready to loop the rope around the cleats and finally attach the rope to the horse. After that was done, Zeeney walked forward and started to lead the horse to the creek bed. The large beast had no problem with the weight and the boat slid easily, finally resting in the creek bed just adjacent to where the boys had determined the trench would be located. With that job complete, they untied the boat from the horse. Zeeney climbed back on the horse to return it to the barn. Toby and Ezra would stay with the boat and start the process of smoothing the final surface. It had been an easy job for the horse, but the boys knew that they could not have moved the heavy boat without him. They could rock the boat over to get to the various surfaces. That was easy, but moving it any distance without the aid of the powerful horse would be impossible.

The rest of Tuesday, and all day Wednesday, were spent working with the scraping tool. Since there was only one tool and three boys, they took turns. They quickly found out that the tool worked best without using any pressure; the weight of the heavy bar alone did the job. It took several passes over each area to create a completely smooth surface, but they were amazed with the beautiful finish it created. Once they painted the boat, it would be perfect. They finished early Wednesday afternoon. After completely admiring their work, they went for a swim. This was the first time Toby and Zeeney ventured out, just slightly, into water that was over their heads, but they quickly moved back to shallow areas of the creek. With each progressive swim they were gaining confidence, but more importantly, they were losing their fear of the water. Ezra felt very proud as a teacher and had no doubt that the boys would be competent swimmers once the boat was launched in just forty-four days.

On Thursday, May 26, they got shovels and picks from the tool shed. The boat was next to the area where the test trench would be which made it easy to approximate the length and width of the trench. The shoreline of the creek bed was surprisingly hard and the boys knew that with the continued clearing and the daily swimming lessons, they would need every bit of the week they had allotted to digging the trench. They wanted it just long, wide, and deep enough to accommodate their new boat.

Finally June 1, 1746 arrived. Summer was only twenty days away and the scheduled launch date was still more than a month away. They began to wonder if they had allotted too much time to this process, but then reassured each other. None of them had ever built a boat before and they did not want to rush the process. Things could still go wrong. The trench was now complete and they were confident that it would accommodate the boat and they could test its reaction to a water environment prior to the official launch. There was a tar pit on the plantation, that all the boys generally avoided because of the rank odor.

A week later, June 7th, they ventured there with each boy carrying a bucket. They had no idea how many buckets would be required, but decided they would revisit the tar pit if necessary. Ezra had carefully marked where he guessed the waterline would be, then he decided to go an inch higher, just in case. They would tar the bottom from that line down and then paint the boat above the line. They agreed to paint the boat dark green and to name it with gold paint. They thought this combination would be appropriate and quite beautiful. The last several days the boys had started to debate a name for the boat, one name that was kicked around was Adventure, another North Point, but in the end Toby and Zeeney felt that the honor went to Ezra because he was the one who originally conceived the boat's creation. Since much of their efforts had been conducted in shady ways, Ezra concluded that there was only one name the boat could have, and the boys unanimously agreed, 'Deception!'

Chapter 24

It took more trips to the tar pit than anticipated, and the boys wanted the tar to cure several days before they started to paint. They intended on several coats of paint but decided that after each coat, they would allow at least forty-eight hours to dry. After each coat dried, they would determine if another coat was necessary. They did not know how the wood would accept the paint, but after the trouble they had gone to assure a smooth surface, they wanted the finish to be as perfect as possible. They had obtained the initial set of paints from Mr. Thomas' woodwork shop; he just added it to the ledger as he had done with the expensive steel scraping bar. At this point, Mr. Thomas wasn't even curious why the boys needed several buckets of dark green paint and a small bucket of gold leaf paint. He just supplied it along with camel hairbrushes and added the cost to the ledger. It took the boys about another week to paint the boat, mainly because of the drying time between coats. The first two coats of paint did not cover all that well so they decided that, to be safe, they would add four coats altogether. After the fourth coat, the boat looked absolutely gorgeous. They decided that they would wait until the paint had completely cured before they named it, and that they would flip the boat over prior to placing the actual name Ezra had chosen, in gold leaf, on the stern of the boat

On Monday, June 15, the boys carefully flipped the boat to its upright position. Even though Ezra had the honor of coming up with the name, it would be Zeeney who would actually paint the name on the boat using the gold leaf paint. Since they were painting over the dark green they knew it would take many coats of the gold leaf in order to cover properly. Zeeney was the most artistic of the three, so the consensus was that Zeeney would have this honor. Ezra would spell out the words on parchment and Zeeney would transcribe the words to the boat. So on Wednesday, June 15, the sailing vessel 'Deception' was officially named. Below 'Deception,' in smaller letters were the words, 'North Point, Maryland.'

Still remaining were the rudder, oars, and outrigger, rigging the boat, flooding the trench, and sliding the boat into the flooded trench. The boys decided that the rudders, oars, and outriggers would be fashioned from the same material as the masts and booms, oak. Again, they decided to rough out these items based on whatever design they agreed on and then deliver them back to the woodwork shop to be finished, stained and varnished. The boat was beautiful; they wanted the rudder, oars, and outrigger to be equally beautiful. It took four days to design and rough out everything. They had not yet decided what they would tell Mr. Thomas these items were when they delivered them back to the woodwork shop, but realized that Mr. Thomas seemed very disinterested in anything they had requested lately. Therefore they might not even try to deceive him again, but rather drop the items off, ask him to add the cost of their production to the ledger, and request an estimated completion date. This was getting far too easy.

They could not believe that the time had actually come to rig the boat. They thought back to the day they saw the masts and booms for the first time, as well as the long walk down the dirt road to deliver the masts and booms to the creek bed. That all seemed so long ago! Now, they were about to retrieve the masts and booms from their hiding place near the shed and bring them to their beautiful new boat. Finally, 'Deception,' would be a sailing vessel.

They knew in advance that the shed held no boring tool that was as large as the masts' diameter. They would have to mark the diameter of the masts at the location of the two raised humps of material they had originally left in the bottom of the boat. They had planned this earlier because they wanted a steady, but strong base in which to place each mast. In addition to the 1-1/4" of hull thickness, they had also left about 6" of a raised hump at each location. They would use the largest boring tool they could find in the shed that would bore four holes within the circle.

They possessed no tool that would create a round hole slightly larger than the hole for the mast, so after boring the four smaller holes they would carefully chisel out the remaining material. This would be in the shape of a square that was only ever so slightly larger than the masts. After the masts were forced into the square hole, they would pack the remaining four spaces with sawdust from Mr. Thomas' woodwork shop. There was plenty of it, as Mr. Thomas had stated, and sawdust wouldn't go on the ledger. As the sawdust was introduced into the spaces around the mast, they would tamp it in layers using the handles of the smallest chisels. Once filled almost to the top, they would fill the remaining space with tar. This would serve two purposes, one, it would waterproof the sawdust, and two, it would look finished. They were determined that every stage of the finishing process would be both functional and attractive.

After holding the shorter of the two masts in place, the boys marked the circle. They had laid the masts opposite each other on the creek bed to make sure that they were exactly the same diameter. To no one's surprise, Mr. Thomas' workmen had done an excellent job and the diameters were identical. Being easier to handle, the shorter of two masts was chosen. After marking the two circles, then using a measuring stick to draw out the squares that completely encompassed the circles. They marked the boring tool at exactly 6" to make sure they did not go past this depth. They found the smallest chisels in the tool shed and started to remove the material within the square, being careful not to remove too much material and to keep their chisels straight up and down. The fit could be tight but not loose. They continually tested the holes dimensions by placing the shorter mast in the hole as they chiseled; this was a tedious, but necessary, process. When both holes were complete they tested the mast in both holes. It was a perfect fit.

The next step was to start to rig the boat. The plan was to use the creek bed as a staging area. They would completely rig both masts lying on the creek bed. Once the masts were complete they would be installed on the boat by carrying them and placing them in their respective holes. They would complete both masts at the same time with one boy dedicating himself to each mast; the remaining boy would go back and forth between the two masts to help each boy. First they attached the blocks they had gone to so much trouble to obtain, by attaching a leather strap and tacking the strap to the mast. They then tacked a series of straps around the mast to give the block a secure hold. When complete, they would glue the final straps, with glue they had also obtained at the woodwork shop, on top of these to hide the tacks. In conjunction with this device, they also added long straps of leather, five to the forward mast, and five to the aft mast. The forward mast would have a forestay that would attach to the bow, two shrouds that would attach to the rails, an outhaul that would attach to the end of the boom for support, and finally a strap that connected the two masts together at their top. This would give the entire rig stability. They had to carefully measure the distance between the two holes that would accept the mast. This would be the distance between the two masts and this strap had to be precise, neither too tight, nor too loose. In the end, they decided to take a chance on slightly tight because they knew that leather stretched and they would not be able to reach this particular strap in the future. They would have to take their chance and hope for the best. The aft mast was being rigged exactly the same way to accept the strap coming from the forward mast, along with two shrouds that would attach to the rails, and two backstays that would attach to each corner where the rails intersected the stern.

All of the ends of the straps, except the one that bridged the two masts, were left loose. They would later be lashed to eyebolts that would be attached to the rail at the appropriate location to accept the stays and shrouds. The eyebolts would allow the crew to tune the rig and retie the straps should they stretch Next, they had to introduce the sails to the appropriate mast. They laid the sails out on the creek bed to assure themselves that the right sail was placed on the right mast. Once they were slid onto the masts from the bottom, they tied a length of rope to the top eyelet in the sail. This rope was run through the block at the top of the mast. Once the masts were in place on the boat, this rope would be used to raise the sails. Later, a cleat would be added to both masts as a tie off point for what the boys would later discover were called halyards. Soon the word rope would disappear from their vocabulary.

Once completed, Ezra and Zeeney picked up the forward mast while Toby handled the aft mast. They carefully lifted the masts. With all the loose ends of leather straps and bulky sails making the job that more difficult, they maneuvered the entire rig toward and into the prepared holes. With some encouragement, the masts were finally in place. They then started to tie off the stays and shrouds to complete that stage of the rigging, but not before they introduced and tamped the sawdust into the spaces surrounding the masts. They decided not to tar the tops of the holes until the rigging was complete and the boat was in the trench. That way, if any flexing of the boat existed while it was on land, it would settle out once in the water. The strap connecting the two masts had apparently been measured correctly. They had to yank on the aft mast to get it to bottom out in the hole, but once in place they could tell that there was no sag in the strap and that the two masts appeared to be parallel. Next, they assembled the booms to the mast. They first fished the boom into and through the pocket that ran from the clew to the tack. Again they used the system they had used at the top of the masts, a series of straps tacked around the mast and then tacked to the boom, then a series of straps around the straps that connected the mast to the boom, all followed by additional straps glued to hide the tacks.

The boom to mast straps were purposely made loose to allow the booms complete freedom of motion so that they would swing freely, from side to side, on any tack. They mounted an eyebolt to the end of each boom to accept the outhaul. Then they attached, as they had done at the top of the masts, blocks at each end of each boom. An eyebolt was attached to the mast, just below the boom. A rope was then tied to the eyelet and fished through the block near the mast at the one at the end of the boom. Later it would be tied to either the starboard or larboard cleat, depending on which tack they were on. A line of rope was attached to the eyelet, known as the clew, and this line was threaded through the block which would later be attached to a cleat that would be added to the underside of the boom once it was finally in place. Their rig was complete.

Chapter 25

The boys discussed raising the sails, but decided that it would not be prudent because the wind, what little there was, blew from the south while the boat pointed west. They did not know much about sailing yet, but knew enough that if they raised the sails in these conditions the boat would most likely fall over. They would leave the sails down until the sea tests took place in the creek. They were all so excited now. They worked at a feverish pace to complete and launch the boat. Finally, it really looked like a sailboat.

These days were devoted only to the completion of the boat; no time was spent on either clearing the creek bed or swimming lessons. In fact, the swimming lessons were over. All three boys felt confident that Toby and Zeeney could swim to shore if tragedy struck and the boat sank. They would always be sure to stay as close as possible to shore as they sailed, this would assure that all three boys could make it safely ashore.

Launch day was quickly approaching. The boys decided that they would wait for the rudder and outriggers to be finished before they slid the boat into the trench. They also realized that the trench was too narrow and would not accommodate the outrigger. Fortunately, they had time too dig it wider. They also needed to figure a way to mount the rudder on the stern. They came up with a simple iron rod that was embedded in the stern rail. This way they could pull the rudder off the stern should they encounter either shallow water or an obstruction. The rudder and tiller assembly would simple pop off the pin. They would make sure that a leather safety strap was adhered to it at all times so that they would not lose the rudder and be unable to steer the boat.

They were almost ready. Once they received the finished items back from Mr. Thomas' shop, nothing was left to do but launch, and that was only three days away. Ezra was slightly excited about his birthday, after all he would be a man come July 8th.. He was far more excited about the launch of 'Deception,' however, and the sea trials in the creek that would follow. He knew that he would have to spend the morning with his family, celebrating his birthday. His afternoon that day would be free, he hoped, and he could meet up with Toby and Zeeney for the real celebration, the official launch of 'Deception.'

On Wednesday, July 6th, Ezra stopped by Mr. Thomas' shop to check on progress.

Mr. Thomas told Ezra that, his items were ready in the finishing room, but that he probably should wait until the next morning to pick them up. Ezra decided he would return in the morning with Toby and Zeeney to pick them up. He also decided that they would not need the horse and cart this time. The three boys could carry all four pieces, the two oars, the rudder, and the outrigger. As usual, on Thursday morning, Toby and Zeeney awaited Ezra's arrival, he had never beaten them.

"Can you believe how close we are?" exclaimed Toby, "Tomorrow we launch 'Deception'."

"No, I can't," replied Ezra. "We've been through so much in such a short time."

"You can say that again!" Zeeney interjected.

They walked through the rooms again toward the finishing room. There was no tour this time and a lack of amazement on the boys' part. The woodworking shop had become old news to them. They entered the finishing room and followed Mr. Thomas to almost the exact spot where the tent poles had formally resided. In typical Mr. Thomas' woodwork shop fashion, the pieces were beautiful. When the boys had initially planned the boat, they pictured something very utilitarian; beauty was not part of the vocabulary they used when discussing the future boat. What had happened, through pure dumb luck, was that they, with a lot of help, had created something truly beautiful. They almost wished they could share its beauty with several people, among them Mr. Thomas, but they knew that was not possible.

They moved down the dirt road as fast as the pieces they carried allowed. Even though they were fatigued, none of the boys asked the others for a break. They just plodded along toward the creek bed.

"Here is the plan," Ezra said. "We will break the dam that separates the creek from the trench. This will flood it. We will place the oars inside 'Deception,' but we won't attach the rudder and affix the outrigger until we slide 'Deception' into the trench."

When they arrived at the creek bed, they quickly sprung into action. First they placed the oars inside the boat, then they dug the dam that separated the creek from the trench. It quickly flooded. They stood on one side and started to push 'Deception' into the flooded trench, first at the bow end and then the stern. They repeated this until finally it tilted and slid into the water. As it slid and rocked back and forth, it splashed into the trench 'Deception' floated for the very first time. A loud cheer resounded simultaneously from the boys. They had done it! The boys jumped into the trench, being careful not to splash any water into 'Deception.' They wanted to assure themselves that the boat was watertight. Not a drop of water appeared anywhere inside the boat, but they would leave 'Deception' in the trench until the next day and test it again. The real test was when the boat bore the weight of the three boys, but that would not come until the sea trials that were just days away. Still anxious to complete their dream, the boys affixed the rudder to the stern pin.

They discovered immediately that the rudder almost popped off the pin as 'Deception' bobbed. This was not going to work. If the rudder nearly came off the pin in the test trench, what would it do in heavy seas? They would approach this problem during the sea trials and come up with a suitable solution.

They then went to work on the outrigger. They had debated earlier as to whether they should mount the outrigger prior to sliding the boat into the trench. When they saw how attractive the outrigger was, they knew that they did not want to take the chance of scratching it. Looking at the rudder, oars, masts, booms, and outrigger, and seeing how truly beautiful they all were, was inspiring. Their choice of the dark green hull and gold leaf lettering only added to the overall beautiful nature of their craft. They had created a truly handsome vessel! The question now was, would it sail? Tomorrow would bring an answer to that question.

It was difficult to affix the outrigger to 'Deception.' They had to stand in the muddy trench and try to steady the rocking boat as Toby affixed the outrigger to the side rails, first one side than the other. Ezra and Zeeney held the boat as best they could as Toby hammered, but it was difficult. Prior to laying the outrigger onto the rails, Toby had pre-bored the nail holes in the outrigger. He determined that this had been a very good idea because the outrigger was very hard to work with and the rails of the outrigger, being round, would be very difficult to pierce on a rocking and unsteady boat. Not only was 'Deception' rocking, but as Toby tried to hold it to the rail, the buoyancy of the outrigger made it almost impossible to hammer the nails into the rail.

Finally, in frustration, Toby said, " This isn't working. If I keep doing it this way, I am going to make a mess of the rails and the outrigger."

They removed the outrigger from the boat and took it back to the creek bed. Staring at it for several minutes Ezra came up with an idea.

"The problem is that every time we strike the nail the boat rocks and one side of the outrigger or the other hits the water. Why don't we do this?" he pondered. "Let's try again, we will hold the outrigger the best we can in place, I'll place the nails almost all the way through the outrigger rail holes. Then if we can really hold it in the right place I will tap the nails to mark the rail. We will do the same on the other side, then we will remove the outrigger altogether. Using the nail impressions as a guide I'll pre-bore the rails just as I did the outrigger. Then I will place nails in all the holes of the outrigger and just through the other side. When we place the outrigger on the rails this time, the exposed nails should fall into the rail holes lining up the outrigger. There may be some scratches on the rail, but they should be covered by the outrigger itself."

"Brilliant idea!" exclaimed Toby and Zeeney. They tried Ezra's plan, and as designed, it did work brilliantly.

The outrigger was now affixed; all three boys were very pleased to see that the boat rocked less noticeably. But in looking at the outrigger, they had some doubts about its design. It was only held in place by four nails, at the conjunction of where the outrigger pole met the rail. Toby felt, and the other boys agreed, that the outrigger might not handle the stresses that were expected of it and its failure might cause the boat to tip over and possibly broach. Toby had already thought of an easy fix. They still had several cleats left after using two for each mast, two for each boom, and four on the rails. They would affix these on the inside of the boat, just below, and in between the rails of the outrigger. This way they could lash the outrigger to the cleats with the remaining leather straps. The orientation of the two cleats on the sides of the boat, parallel to the rail, would assure that the outrigger would be very secure.

As they stood there admiring their work no one said a thing until finally Zeeney commented, "we did it. 'Deception' is a sailboat!"

Since the boat was rigged and in the trench, there was no way to hide it any longer. They decided that from that point further they would just have to take their chances and hope that no one came across the boat.

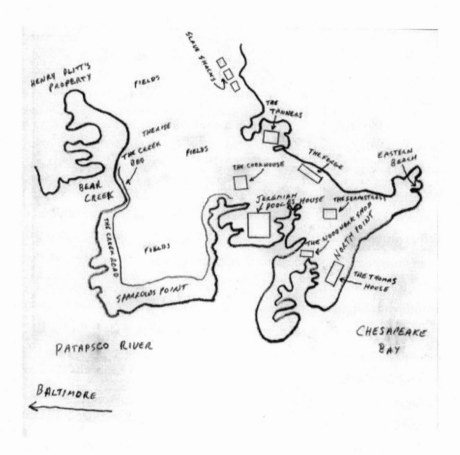

Chapter 26

THE LAUNCH

On Friday, July 8, 1746, Ezra was thirteen years old, a man. As he awoke, he thought of the difficulty he had falling asleep the night before. He was not looking at all forward to his "birthday party;" he was sure they would "surprise" him with one this morning His family had done the same thing on every birthday that Ezra could remember. Father took off work that day and the entire family would celebrate Ezra's birthday. This had always been very special to Ezra because this was his day. In fact, Ezra knew of no other person that shared his birthday. He had previously asked Toby and Zeeney about their birthdays, but they just shrugged their shoulders. As far as either one of them knew, they did not have birthdays. At one time he had argued the point with them, but each year he got the same reaction. When he finally suggested that all three boys share the same birthday, the discussion was over.

On this particular birthday, the one when he would be come a man, Ezra had one thought, 'Deception!' All he wanted to do was get through all of the party festivities and head to his boat. He would sail it for the very first time that day. When he entered the main room of the house, his entire family was gathered there. His father had seen fit to even invite Toby and Zeeney to the party. They were as "thick as thieves," and Mr Pooles did not want to separate them. Little did he know how truly apt his description was.

The Pooles family loved birthdays and each member got the same treatment Mr. Pooles was very fortunate that, except for Ezra, all other birthdays were in winter months when planting and harvesting was done. Otherwise, he might not have liked these family activities as much. They took away almost an entire day of managing the plantation. Jeremiah was family-oriented but he did have a plantation to run. Ezra knew this as well as the fact that his father would eventually tire of these activities and return to his duties.

Ezra's birthday would be treated the same as any other member of the family but this particular birthday was significant in that Ezra was turning thirteen. As he had done with all of Ezra's older brothers, Father would announce at the height of the festivities the manly duties Ezra was about to attain. This Ezra could wait for!

Since Ezra was the birthday boy, he would be the center of attention that day, a role he did not relish. When he walked into the main room, he saw all of his family and friends gathered there to celebrate this day. He was surprised to see Elizabeth there as well and tried to avoid her. Anna May had gone to extra efforts to make all the goodies that Ezra liked, as he walked around the table, he was pursued by Elizabeth.

"Happy birthday Ezra," she greeted him.

"Thank you," replied Ezra.

"By the way," she continued with a whisper, "how did the tent come out? Grandfather tells me the poles turned out quite nicely."

Ezra just shrugged his shoulders; he really did not want to discuss the non-existent tent, especially where his family members might hear.

"Happy birthday!" chimed Toby and Zeeney.

"And happy birthday to you two as well!"

Toby and Zeeney glanced at each other and smiled, they had forgotten of their agreement with Ezra to share his birthday, since this was the first time they were confused on what to do.

Toby glanced at Zeeney, "happy birthday Zeeney," Zeeney looked back at Toby, "yeah, and happy birthday to you." They both just smiled.

Again Ezra replied, "happy birthday to all three of us."

"What time do you think we'll get out of here?" Asked Toby.

"I don't know, soon I hope, Father has to give his speech, then things will wind down. I hope we can get to the creek bed and have some time this afternoon."

"Time for what?" Elizabeth inquired. Ezra wished she would just go away, but since she was obviously going to shadow him he would have to deal with her.

"Toby, Zeeney and I have work at the creek bed down at Bear Creek," Ezra answered.

"We're going to leave here as soon as the party is over."

"Can I come?" asked Elizabeth. "Grandfather told me about the unusual things he is building for you. A boat I understand?"

"Be quiet about that," blurted Ezra. Then he wondered who else Mr. Thomas might have told.

Elizabeth continued, "Well, I love boats and would love to go on your boat with you."

"There is no boat, only boat parts. Father wants a boatyard at the creek bed, and we are getting it ready. Do me a favor, will you? Just like the tent, don't mention boats to anyone!"

Elizabeth seemed a little stunned by his remarks. She really thought that Ezra was fond of her, and she had done everything she could to help him. Her demeanor changed and her smile returned.

"Alright," she whispered. "It will be our little secret, but as soon as you get your boat, I want a ride."

Mr. Pooles was starting to raise his voice. "Family and friends," he repeated, each time a little louder to get everyone's attention. Eventually the buzz of conversation in the great room died down and Mr. Pooles had the floor.

"Family and friends," he continued one more time. "Today my son becomes a man, and as is the tradition in the Pooles family, on this day I announce the duties of the new man in the family. I am very proud of Ezra. Even before today he has shown the makings of a man. Why, already this spring, well before his birthday, Ezra came to me and asked that he and his good friends here, Toby and Zeeney, could be allowed to clear the creek bed. You all may not know this, but I have always pictured Bear Creek as the perfect place for a boatyard, a place where boats could be built and maintained. I have no idea how Ezra knew of this and shared my dream, but I am very proud of him and the work he has already completed with Toby and Zeeney. As a man, I have decided that his first responsibility will be to continue his work there and that someday we will have a functioning boatyard at North Point Plantation."

Toby and Zeeney glanced at Ezra. Ezra just raised his hand upwards in a gesture of amazement. Little did Mr. Pooles know that he already had a working boatyard.

Mr. Pooles continued, "In addition to Toby and Zeeney, I am assigning other men to Ezra as his work crew, and his new responsibilities will begin tomorrow! Congratulations and happy birthday."

As the applause in the room broke out and then slowly diminished, Ezra, Toby, and Zeeney rushed to each other. When Mr. Pooles saw this he assumed they were offering their congratulations.

"What are we going to do?" asked Zeeney.

"I don't know," replied Ezra, "but we had better think of something fast."

They were going to launch the boat that afternoon as planned, but now everything was on hold and Father would easily find out what the boys had actually been doing all Spring. Their goose was truly cooked!

"We'll meet at the boat as soon as this party winds down, then we'll think of something. We can't hide it. Heck, we don't even know how to sail it."

The party did eventually wind down and the boys, headed toward the boat. The elation they were sure this day would bring was completely gone. They walked silently. This was the first time no one had a plan. It was over. They would be found out tomorrow and they would all be punished, maybe severely. Then, Ezra showed them something he had borrowed from the house before the shock of his father's announcement. It was a bottle wrapped in burlap.

"What's that?" asked Zeeney.

"Well," replied Ezra, " I thought we were going to celebrate and christen 'Deception.' It's hard cider but I guess we'll just drink it instead."

"Let's christen it anyway. It's probably our last day with the boat so let's enjoy it just the same and deal with our problem tomorrow," Zeeney said.

"Yes, I guess you're right," replied Ezra.

They should have all felt better, but they really didn't. They would pretend anyway, but each knew no one was fooled.

When they arrived at 'Deception,' they did the christening ceremony first, although none of the boys knew how to conduct a christening. Toby and Zeeney didn't really understand what a christening was, but they went along anyway. Standing in the muddy trench, with water up above their knees, they began. They all gathered at the bow, for some reason, this seemed more appropriate than the stern.

"Well, here goes," said Ezra. "I think we should drink some first before we begin."

He passed the bottle of strong spirits to Toby first. Toby took a swig and, as he gasped for air, passed it to Zeeney, who swigged and choked as the strong concoction hit his throat Zeeney passed the bottle back to Ezra, who took the last swallow before the actual ceremony started.

"You've been a good boat for the short time we have had you," Ezra started. "Looks like the only sailing you will do is what we do today because I'm sure my father will have you destroyed tomorrow. We're going to name you anyway, so here goes. I christen you 'Deception'."

With that proclamation Ezra swung the bottle wrapped in burlap as hard as he could, trying to strike the cleat on the bow and not the rail. Even though he knew the boat was not going to be around much longer, he did not want to be the one to damage it. When the thin bottle hit the cleat it broke easily and the remaining cider ran down the side of 'Deception.' It was finally time to sail.

Chapter 27

THE ADVENTURE

Toby and Zeeney were excited, but nervous. They decided that Ezra should have the honor of the first sail. They would guide 'Deception' at first, into the deeper water to get Ezra going in the right direction. Ezra did not really have a clue of what to do, but he had dreamt of this day every day since the initial inception of the boat. Ezra did know that he was going to sail with only the head, or front sail, initially until he was accustomed to handling the rig. They would probably not use the aft sail until most of the sea trials were complete and both Toby and Zeeney were on board. As he thought this, he realized that there probably were not going to be any further sea trials. What was he thinking?

"Well," he thought out loud, "I might as well enjoy this."

He raised the headsail.

As soon as he tried to raise the sail, the boat started to react erratically. He realized that 'Deception' was faced westerly and the light wind was out of the south. Toby and Zenney still held to the sides and were still in water where they could stand. This helped, but there had to be a better solution.

"Quick!" said Ezra. "Can you turn 'Deception' into the wind?"

"Where's the wind?" asked Toby.

Ezra pointed south. The two boys in the water guided 'Deception' to the left. This took the pressure off of the sail and Ezra was easily able to pull the headsail to the top of the gorgeous oak mast with the block arrangement they had affixed to the top. He held a rope in his hand that the boys would later know as the mainsheet. It was attached to the boom and would allow the boys to position the boom according to wind direction. The fully raised head sail now rattled in the wind, but because it was directly facing south, no longer pressured the sail.

"Alright," said Ezra, " slowly turn me back toward the other side of the creek."

They did, as he said. As the sail filled with wind, the mainsheet pulled from Ezra's hands. The boom swung all the way to the right and was only stopped by the leather shroud that ran from the top of the mast to the rail on the right side of the boat. But more importantly, Ezra was sailing!

His first sail did not last long. He had concentrated all of his attention to dealing with the headsail and completely disregarded the rudder; therefore the boat was steering itself. 'Deception' traveled very quickly and left Toby and Zeeney in its wake. As they watched helplessly, Ezra and 'Deception' raced quickly across the narrow creek and stopped with a loud thud as the boat hit the opposite shoreline. Toby and Zeeney did not have to test their newly learned swimming skills that day as this part of the creek was fairly shallow.

"Wow, you went really fast! What happened?"

Ezra, laughing, said, "I forgot to steer. We have to do the first modification to the boat. I can't hold the mainsheet, its too much pressure."

"What's a mainsheet?" queried Toby.

Ezra answered him, " I found some old books on sailing ships in Father's library. One of them names all the parts of a sailboat, and we'll have to learn them. Did you know, for instance, there are no ropes on a sailboat? Each one has a name based on its function"

"Why do we have to learn the names of parts of the boat if we will never sail it again?" asked Zeeney.

"Good point," replied Ezra. " Let's head back to the other shore, modify the boat and try again."

"How are we going to modify it?" asked Toby, as Ezra dropped the headsail and they walked the boat back to the trench.

"We have some cleats left, don't we?" asked Ezra. "We'll put one on each rail right about here," he pointed to the rail.

"We'll put another set back at the aft sail, otherwise we will never be able to hold the sails. Once they are set properly we can cleat the mainsheet off and the cleat will do the work."

"What's a mainsheet again?" Toby asked. Ezra pointed to the rope hanging from the boom. Quickly Zeeney raced to the shed to fetch four cleats, a hammer and nails, and a boring tool.

"We are going through these cleats so fast," he thought, "we're going to have to find some more real soon." He returned and they quickly made the modifications.

"Alright, let's try again," he shouted.

"This time, steer," said Zeeney. They set the boat up exactly the same, turning into the wind as Ezra raised the headsail. This time, as soon as the sail was raised, he did a single wrap around the rail cleat and reached back for the tiller.

"Alright, turn her away from the wind."

The sail was tugged by the wind, but this time the cleat held the mainsheet and not Ezra's hand. 'Deception' shot from Toby and Zeeney's grasp. Ezra was really sailing now. He moved the rudder to force the boat in a more southeasterly direction, and he pulled the mainsheet in to grab more of the wind, tying it off with the cleat when it was set to his satisfaction. This time he felt in control, he was now sailing parallel to the shoreline. It was going to be a beautiful sail. Toby and Zeeney watched with glee as 'Deception' quickly moved away. But as the watched, they wondered why Ezra was drifting toward the opposite shoreline. He was steering, even forcing the rudder in the other direction, but 'Deception' did not respond. Soon there was another thud, this time not the bow, but the side of the boat. Toby and Zeeney crossed to the other side then walked down the shoreline. Ezra was very pleased that he sailed, but had a perplexed look on his face.

"No matter what I did," exclaimed Ezra, " the boat just kept drifting to the shore, the rudder didn't help!"

"Maybe the rudder isn't big enough," suggested Toby.

"I don't think that's it," replied Ezra. "Let's take her back and try to figure what's wrong! We can't all be in the boat if we can't control the direction she heads."

Toby and Zeeney again turned the boat back toward the trench as Ezra dropped the sail.

Chapter 28

When Ezra awoke the next morning, as he was rolling over in bed, he thought, "The boat is done before we even got started. I couldn't even sail her properly!"

He just had to think of something. That morning his father would assign men to work on the boatyard project. Once they saw the boat already there, they would be sure to report back to Mr. Pooles. At the very least, Father would be unhappy with Ezra and would most likely severely punish him for the deception. There just had to be a way! Ezra thought hard as he lay in his bed.

"Well," he thought, nothing to lose. I'll give it one more shot."

Ezra entered his father's office and greeted him, "Good morning."

"Good morning, Son," replied his father. "Big day today for you, Son."

"Yes sir," replied Ezra. "I was thinking about the boatyard project you have assigned me. I really appreciate the honor and trust you have in me to take on such an ambitious project, but I have a request."

"Yes, what is that, Son?"

Ezra continued. "The three of us, myself, Toby and Zeeney, haven't worked as hard as you think doing the clearing job that you agreed to allow us to do. I should have admitted to you that we have wasted a lot of time."

"Doing what?" asked his father.

"Well, mostly swimming when we should have been working," replied Ezra.

"Well, Son, I can understand that, but now that you have the responsibility of managing a larger crew and having men instead of boys to supervise all of that will change."

"Yes, Sir, I understand that, but I have a request."

"And what would that be?" inquired his father.

"I would like you to postpone the assignment of the crew to allow me to get the original part of the project done. I'm sure you really can't afford to pull men from planting at this busy time. I can assure you that if you allow us to finish, we will accomplish the job quickly."

"How long do you think that would be?" asked his father.

"Oh, I'm not sure, but at least another month."

"Another month!" exclaimed his father. You certainly have been doing a lot of swimming!"

"Yes, Sir, and I feel really badly about it and wanted to make it up to you, especially after the nice things you said on my birthday."

"Alright then, but you report back to me in two weeks, and I want to hear some progress, and no swimming, or at least very little. I want that job done."

"Yes, Sir," said Ezra. "We'll start today and report back in three weeks."

"Two weeks," replied his father, in a rather stern manner.

"Yes, Sir, two weeks. I'll get it done."

Ezra left his father's office. He felt somewhat better, but knew this was a temporary reprieve. Now he had to tackle the sailing problem. Ezra returned to his father's library to refer to the book where he was learning the parts of a sailing vessel.

"Maybe the answer is in here," he thought as he paged through the book. As he flipped through the pages, he found a section named,

'Anatomy of a Sailing Vessel,' and he read it. It discussed the dynamics and forces that affect a sailing vessel. He found exactly what he was looking for.

The force of the wind on the sails of a sailing vessel from any quarter other than the stern will not have the desired effect without the resistance of the keel against the water; without a keel the boat will obtain an uncontrolled drift toward the leeward side. With a keel, of sufficient size, the force of the wind against the sails will create a forward, rather than a sideways, motion of the boat.

That was it! He couldn't believe he had found the answer so easily and so quickly. A keel! But how were they to add one? They couldn't have incorporated one to the original design. The tree was barely thick enough to allow for the boat they had now, and they did not have the tools or the knowledge to add one to the hull. The last thing he wanted to do was cut a hole in the bottom, but it was clear that, without a keel, they could not sail the boat with any control unless they were downwind all the time. Ezra knew that with the finicky nature of the bay, they would not have the luxury of always sailing downwind. He felt that their sailing would most likely be more to windward and that the present design would not work. He had some good, but temporary, news for Toby and Zeeney and he was anxious to tell them. He also knew that the three of them could solve just about any problem. They had so far!

When Ezra arrived at the creek bed, Toby and Zeeney were very surprised to see him alone. They were just sitting there contemplating the trouble they were all in. They did not even try to cover up the boat because they knew it was futile.

"Good news! Well, temporary good news. I've convinced my father that because we have been so lazy, he should postpone assigning a crew to work on the yard."

"How did you do that?" asked Toby.

"Well, a little more deception, but we only have a month. I have to report on our progress in two weeks so we had better get going. Also, I referred to the sailing book and found out our drifting problem, but I don't know the solution. We need to work on one."

Ezra related to the boys what he had discovered from the book and also told them why he did not think they could modify the hull.

After a period of time, Zeeney said, " Besides the hull, the only other parts that touch the water are the rudder and the outrigger. Making the rudder larger won't do it, so we will have to modify the outrigger. Wait while I get some parchment and coal, maybe we can come up with a design that will work."

Zeeney ran back to the shed to gather up the parchment and coal. Before he arrived back at the boat, he already had a design in mind. He sat back on the ground and scribbled out a rough design, drawing a front view of the boat. He drew keels* extending from the bottom of each outrigger.

"That won't work," Toby and Ezra both said.

"Why not?" asked Zeeney.

"Well," Toby continued. "It will take weeks for us to cut out a new outrigger and have Mr. Thomas finish it for us, we'll have to cut down another very large oak. No, that plan won't work."

"What I was thinking of was a modification to the existing design. We already have enough oak left over from the original cutting of the oak tree. We will just have to get. Mr. Thomas to finish the keels[1] and cut slots in the original outrigger that we can slide the keels into. That will only take a few days, maybe less if loverboy here can sweet talk Elizabeth again," Zeeney replied, poking Ezra in the arm.

---

[1]Keels were, in fact, removable daggerboards, but that word did not yet exist, therefore the boys referred to the two daggerboards as keels

"Alright, this may work after all, and while we are waiting we can get the rest of the clearing done," Toby said.

"Let's do it!" responded Ezra.

They quickly returned to the scrap pile and found enough oak to do the job. The pieces were long enough, but not wide enough. Mr. Thomas would have to use his skills to connect the pieces. Zeeney would redraw the plan, this time to scale, as Toby and Ezra rough cut the pieces. When they were done they hustled to the woodwork shop to drop them off and beg Mr. Thomas to complete them quickly. Getting the outrigger off the boat was very easy. After they removed the lashes that connected to cleats, the device lifted off the rails with ease. This reinforced the boys original belief that simply nailing the outrigger to the rails would not work. Luckily, Mr. Thomas informed the boys that they were caught up on their work and could start on the modifications right away. Ezra was immediately relieved; he did not have to have contact with Elizabeth

"Of course, there will be a charge for this modification," Mr. Thomas stated

"Put it on the ledger," the three boys said in unison. After dropping off the outrigger and pieces for the new keels, they raced back to the creek bed. This time they wouldn't mind clearing.

'Deception'

Chapter 29

Today was the day! Ezra was confident that he would sail 'Deception' that day for the very first time without problems, he hoped. When he arrived at the woodworking shop, Toby and Zeeney were already waiting. Mr. Thomas led the boys, as usual, back to the finishing room, and as usual, the modifications were complete and beautifully done. Mr. Thomas reached down and picked up one of the new keels.

"The pieces were cut to length and then we cut dovetail joints into the opposing pieces. We glued the joints and then clamped them together. After they dried, we added this handle at the top, which will also act as a stop to keep the pieces from sliding through the outrigger. We then cut slots into the existing outrigger, slightly larger than the blades themselves. Afterwards we finished all the pieces," he explained. "I guess once you boys actually have me build you a boat, you'll have something to use these on?"

"Yes, Sir," replied Ezra.

The boys grabbed the modified outrigger pieces and headed back to the creek, they could not hide their excitement. If this worked, and they had no doubt it would, not only would Ezra be able to sail, but Toby and Zeeney might even join him. They would go through the same routine as days before. Ezra would climb into the boat while Toby and Zeeney guided it from the trench to the deeper creek. As soon as they arrived, they placed the outrigger back on the boat. This was very easy, as the nail holes already existed. They finished lashing the outrigger to the cleats with leather straps and were prepared to set sail. Ezra had the new keels, which were just over four feet long, with him inside the boat. He knew that they were too long to install in the trench so he would wait until he was in deeper water. Once Toby and Zeeney were in water about chest deep he placed first one keel, then the other, in the slots. Immediately he realized there was a problem. They fit perfectly, but as soon as he inserted them in the slots and released his hand from the handles on top of each keel, they popped up and nearly out of the slots.

"This isn't going to work," he thought. He stared at the popping keels for a brief moment and said, "We will have to come up with a temporary fix for this problem. Toby, run to the shed and bring some more leather straps, we'll tie these down temporarily until we get back in and can figure a permanent solution. I want to sail!"

Toby ran to the shed, but was back in a flash. Ezra, with Toby and Zeeney's help, lashed down one keel and then another. Finally they were ready.

Toby and Zeeney headed 'Deception' into the wind; they finally understood from which direction the wind blew. As they turned the boat, Ezra slowly started to raise the forward, or headsail.

"Alright," he said, "I'm ready."

As the boys turned the boat away from the wind direction, the sail picked up the wind and Ezra was off. This time the boat answered to the rudder and Ezra was able to control the boat's direction. It had worked! Although there was still a little drift this time Ezra could control the course of the boat. Finally, he was sailing! As 'Deception' built up speed, Ezra decided to play with the steering a little. As he headed west toward the river, he discovered that his movement was somewhat limited. He could steer slightly left, or what he discovered in his sailing book was larboard, before the sail began to rattle and he lost speed. If he went to the right, or starboard, he would steer into the opposite creek shoreline. Toby and Zeeney were now quite far in the distance yelling and waving to Ezra.

"Time to go back to them," he thought but he did not know how to turn the boat around. Then he remembered a discussion in his sailing book about something called tacking, used to change direction. Since he could see that the mouth of the deeper river was not all that far away and Toby and Zeeney were disappearing in the distance, now was the time. As he turned the rudder toward shore, the boat turned back toward the wind and then through it. Ezra observed that the sail twisted the boom from the starboard to the larboard side. The mainsheet was still tied to the cleat on the starboard rail. Ezra knew he had to release it and cleat it to the other side. It was quite difficult trying to handle the rudder and the mainsheet at the same time, but he was able to accomplish this feat and was now headed back toward the boys. He was also picking up the speed he had lost during the tack. Toby and Zeeney grew larger as he approached, and they were still waving and yelling. He finally reached them and was moving at a pretty good pace.

"I don't know how to stop!" he yelled as he slid by. He was headed back toward shallow water. He knew that eventually the rising creek bottom would stop his forward motion, but he didn't want to damage their brand new boat.

"How do I stop this thing?" he quickly wondered.

He remembered that the boat could not make any forward movement into the wind, and that was the direction he headed when he wanted to raise the sails. He decided the best course of action, was to release the main halyard, which held the sail up the mast, and head directly into the wind. As soon as he did both, the boat almost came to a complete stop.

Toby and Zeeney, splashing a lot of water as they ran toward the boat, screeched, "Ezra, you sailed, you did it! How did you know how to stop?"

"It just came to me," he said. We are really going to have to understand the wind better in order to sail the boat. We also should practice here in the creek before we venture into deeper water. How about it, you two, want to go sailing?"

"Yes!" screamed both Toby and Zeeney.

Zeeney climbed in. Toby held the boat into the wind as Ezra re-raised the headsail. Once it was up, Toby drifted the boat away from the wind as he climbed in. The new Captain, Ezra, started to explain to the boys the procedure. They would simply sail back and forth on the creek sailing from east to west and then back again. They would do this repeatedly to learn how to handle the boat, each taking turns steering and handling the mainsheet. Ezra explained to the boys what he understood about tacking as well as how he discovered just how to stop the boat's forward movement. He also explained how dangerous the boom appeared to be when it swung from one side of the boat to the other during a tack, especially with all three aboard and at least one of the crew sitting below that boom, they would have to be aware of its movement. For the rest of that day, they tacked back and forth on the creek. It never became boring or monotonous. They were sailing! And for the first time, all the boat's functions seemed to work properly. They decided that until they were more knowledgeable as a crew, they would only raise the headsail; the aft sail would be used once they were more experienced.

Chapter 30

It was day two of sailing 'Deception' and the boys felt it was as natural as walking, Bear Creek ran from east to west emptying into the Patapsco River. Once on the Patapsco, it was a short distance to the Chesapeake Bay to larboard and a longer distance to Baltimore Town to starboard. The boys had already tired of the constant tacking back and forth on Bear Creek. They could sail shore to shore, although the distance was very short, and they felt experienced enough to handle short tacks should something go wrong. But even on the second day of sailing, they were anxious to move to the next step. Up to this point, all their sailing had been a beam reach, that is, on each tack the wind was exactly on their beam. Ezra told Toby and Zeeney that they needed to find out what 'Deception' was capable of on other points of sail. In their short experience sailing, the wind always blew out of the south, and as far as they knew, the wind must always blow from the south on the Chesapeake. Therefore, Ezra surmised, if they were to find out what 'Deception' was capable of on other points of sail, they would have to venture out to the Patapsco itself. Since Toby and Zeeney could now swim and did not fear the water, they would try. They would follow their original plan and be careful to stay as close to land as possible. Before they pushed 'Deception' out into the creek from its home in the trench, Ezra drew a diagram in the sand on the beach.

"Here is Bear Creek. It runs from east to west, it runs into the Patapsco here. I'm not sure how far it is to the opposite shore but I know it is far. When I was younger and Mother would take me to the Eastern Beach, she told me it was the Chesapeake Bay, all I could tell was that it was very large. The Chesapeake is to the left on the Patapsco, and Baltimore Town is to the right. We may never see Baltimore Town by water, but we will head toward the Chesapeake on our adventure." Ezra drew more details in the sand.

"The wind always blows from the south, I guess that is what it always does." He drew an arrow representing the wind pointing toward and perpendicular to Bear Creek. He explained to Toby and Zeeney, "I read in the sailing book in Father's library that there are different points, or directions, of sail based on the prevailing wind direction. Just as we need to learn the proper terms for the parts of boat, we also need to learn the points of sail so that we can easily communicate. We already discovered that the only way we can raise the sails or stop the boat is to head the bow directly into the wind, this is called 'in irons.'"

Ezra picked up a stick lying nearby that had a knob at one end.

"Let's suppose that this stick is 'Deception' and this knob is the bow." He laid it on the sand. " In this direction, facing the wind is 'in irons.' According to Father's sailing book, there are four points of sail on each side of the boat. At 40 degrees of either side of the wind direction is 'close hauled'," he moved the stick 40 degrees from the arrow. " In between 40 and 90 degrees, we are on a 'close reach.' At 90 degrees," he turned the stick perpendicular to the arrow, "we are at a 'beam reach.' This is the point of sail we were on all day yesterday." He turned the stick again between 90 degrees and 135 degrees.

"This is a 'broad reach." Finally Ezra turned the stick directly opposite the arrow that represented the wind, with the bow facing away from the wind. "This is a 'run,' directly down wind. Except for the 'in irons' and the 'run,' each point of sail is repeated on both sides, larboard and starboard."

Toby and Zeeney looked down at the drawing in the sand and the stick that Ezra said represented 'Deception.' They then looked at each other, then at the drawing again.

Toby finally said, "Well, this looks harder than learning English." He remembered how hard it was to learn the strange language they spoke today when their people still spoke the language they could not remember.

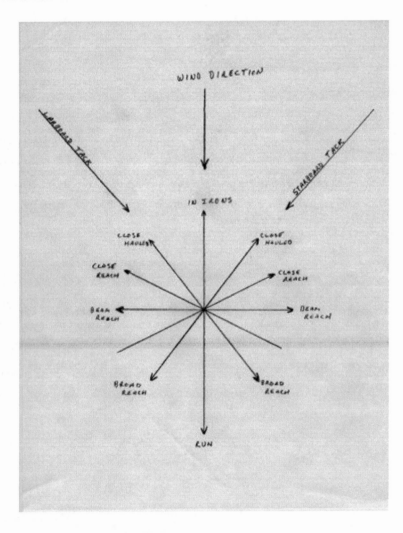

"We're not going to learn this," Toby protested.

"Sure we will," replied Ezra. "Once we start to sail, it should come natural. We'll just have to take small steps, like we did with swimming lessons. What we should do is yell the point of sail we are on when we change direction; it is the only way we will learn. Only problem is that the wind is always out of the south. If we don't leave Bear Creek, we'll never experience the different points of sail, and we really have to do that to learn."

"You mean leave Bear Creek and go out on the Patapsco?" asked Zeeney.

"That's right," replied Ezra, "and I think we should do it today."

The boys pushed 'Deception' from the trench into the creek. Today Zeeney was the captain and Ezra and Toby pushed the boat as crew. They decided that it was only fair, since they were equal partners, that each day a different member of the crew would be named captain and call out the orders. Until they learned the points of sail, however, they would all shout out the new point when they changed directions. Zeeney placed the keels in the outrigger when they were in deep enough water. Toby and Ezra helped him lash the keels in place; they had not yet addressed a better solution. They were ready to go. As always the wind was from the south and Toby and Zeeney twisted 'Deception' in the water facing the bow to the wind as Zeeney raised the headsail. Once it was up and as the boys pushed 'Deception' away from the wind, they jumped in and the boat took off down Bear Creek. This was the first time anyone other that Ezra had steered the boat and it was obvious the Zeeney was enjoying the experience. They had an easy 'beam reach' all the way down Bear Creek. Until they entered the Patapsco they could not have imagined how large a body of water it was. Even when they had walked down the dirt road to the creek they had not appreciated how large the river was. Now that they were on the river in their small craft, they were aware of how large the river truly was. They were all frightened, but none of them said a word.

Once they reached the mouth of Bear Creek, they were free to sail something other than a 'beam reach.' They headed to larboard and had to tighten the mainsheet to bring the boom closer amidships. Toby, Zeeney, and Ezra all yelled, "close hauled"

Ezra yelled back to Zeeney on the tiller, "Captain, why don't we raise the aft sail?"

"Let's do it," replied Zeeney. "Head to wind!"

As soon as 'Deception' was 'in irons,' Zeeney raised the aft sail. For the very first time, they were sailing 'Deception' with both sails. It was exhilarating! They then dropped off the wind and back to "close hauled," It occurred to Zeeney that now that they were free from the confines of Bear Creek, they should probably take 'Deception' through its paces and hit every point of sail. Zeeney slowly moved the tiller to the left. As soon as he reached the next point, Toby and Ezra yelled back to him, "Beam reach!"

Oh the fun they were having! All the work was worth it, they loved to sail!

Zeeney moved the tiller to the left again, but he noticed that 'Deception' was leaning very far to starboard. He gave the order to ease the mainsheets, and the boat came more upright.

"Broad reach," they yelled.

"One more point and we should head back," Zeeney ordered. He liked being Captain. Turning the tiller more to the left again, Captain Zeeney ordered, "Release the mainsheets!" The boys followed his order and they realized that they were now on a 'run.'

The aft sail seemed to be doing all the work. The headsail rattled when they were too close to the wind. The boys did not understand this, but they were still moving. To the right Zeeney could see Bear Creek was fading away and he did not want to go too far up the Patapsco. He pulled the tiller to the left and ordered his crew to tighten the main sheets. Suddenly, the aft sail, then the headsail boom, slid to larboard with a bang. They had experienced their first jibe. They were now back on 'close hauled' and headed directly toward Bear Creek. Zeeney loved handling the tiller. He could feel the power and adjust the speed of the boat through slight movements. He was not going to be as good a crewman after handling the tiller and giving the orders. He loved this!

Back in Bear Creek and now back on a 'beam reach,' Zeeney headed the boat back up Bear Creek and to the trench. The boys all commented on how much fun the sail had been and how well 'Deception' had performed. Toby and Ezra also agreed that Zeeney seemed to be a natural captain. They were impressed. When they were back to the trench, Zeeney pushed the tiller abruptly to larboard; the boat shot up into the wind and came to an almost immediate stop.

Next it was Toby's turn to be Captain. He traded places with Zeeney at the tiller. Toby thought steering the boat would be easy; Zeeney had just done it perfectly on his first try. But Toby was nervous and he was confused by the action of the tiller. Everything seemed backwards to him. This time only Ezra jumped out to get the boat back into the wind. He suggested to Toby that he might want to start with just the headsail. Toby nervously agreed and released the aft sail halyard. As 'Deception' caught the wind with Captain Toby at the tiller, Ezra jumped back on the boat. 'Deception' was still sailing very close to the wind and Toby knew that he wanted to be on a 'beam reach' as Zeeney had been when he navigated west on Bear Creek. He quickly pushed the tiller away from him to starboard, but instead of getting the results he expected, the boat headed back into the wind and came to a stop. No movement of the rudder had any affect; the sail rattled and the boat slowly drifted toward the far shore.

"We're in 'irons!'" exclaimed Ezra.

"What's that?" Toby yelled, as he frantically moved the rudder back and forth with no reaction from the boat.

"I'll explain later," Ezra said. "Place the rudder amidships while I jump over the side. I'll hold the stern and kick with my legs. As soon as the wind fills the sail again help me back in, but Toby, hold the rudder where it is until I am back in the boat."

Toby answered affirmatively and Ezra went over the side. Soon the wind was back in the single sail and they were slowly moving away from the far shore. Zeeney helped Ezra back into the boat. Toby held firmly onto the rudder fearing that another wrong move on his part would put them back in 'irons' again.

"What's 'irons'?" Toby asked Ezra.

Ezra responded, "I also found this term in the sailing book when I was studying points of sail. If the boat is too close to the wind on either a larboard or starboard tack, and it is steered closer rather than away from the wind, what just happened will occur, and the boat will be 'in irons.' According to the book, getting out of 'irons' is nearly impossible and requires an action like the one we just took. On larger sailing vessels, the crew has to enter rowboats attached to the larger sailing vessel and attempt to row the ship out of 'irons.' You can imagine how unpopular the helmsman of the ship is with the crew."

This was just what Toby did not want to hear, but unfortunately he would place the boat into 'irons' two more times. He just could not get the hang of that rudder. They finally struggled back to the trench, but when it was time to turn the boat up into the wind to stop it, Toby again turned the wrong way and they were headed downwind instead.

"Pull the tiller toward you!" Zeeney and Ezra both yelled.

As Toby did this, the boat made an abrupt turn and was back in 'irons,' this time, however, this was where he wanted it to be.

Toby went forward and Ezra positioned himself as Captain. It was his turn now. His sail was completely uneventful. Not as flawless as Zeeney's sail, but far better than Toby's. Ezra got in 'irons' one time and one time only, and he successfully got into 'irons,' at the completion of the sail when he returned to the trench. It was obvious to all of the boys that Zeeney was the natural captain. Both Ezra and Zeeney tried to console Toby, after all it was their first try. They would all get better with practice.

When 'Deception' was safely back in the trench and the boys were back on land, Ezra suggested that they work on the creek bed while they planned their next move.

"Is anyone still rocking or is it just me?" Zeeney asked.

"Yes," replied both Ezra and Toby.

"I thought that was just something strange that only happened to me!" exclaimed Ezra.

"It must be something related to being on the water, I sure feel dizzy!"

As they walked back to the creek bed, Ezra continued, "I was looking at the calendar the other day and I think this coming Saturday, July 16th would be a perfect day to start our adventure. I think I can come up with an excuse to get us away for several nights. My two weeks report is coming up on the 22nd. I think we can use that to our advantage, but we had better get a lot of clearing done between now and the 16th, just in case."

Chapter 31

The week before the start of their adventure went by quickly. The boys all had jobs to do besides clearing the creek bed. Ezra had already met with his father again, and convinced him that he and his crew were not making the progress he had expected. He asked if it would be all right if they camped at the creek bed for several nights. This would allow them to work longer each day and start earlier each morning. They would also like to get some non-perishable food from Anna May. This way they could work through meals and not lose time on meal breaks. Jeremiah was pleased and impressed with Ezra's initiative.

"That's fine, son," he said, "but don't forget that you are to report to me, when?" Ezra's father glanced at the calendar. "Oh, yes, the 22nd of July, that would be the two-week mark from when you requested an extension. I expect to hear great progress that day."

"Oh, yes, Sir, you will, Sir!"

Now Ezra had his alibi. The three boys could disappear for several days without being missed. They only had to get their supplies, food, and a change of clothes for the adventure. It was actually about to happen! He didn't have a clue what he would tell his father when the month was up, but he had other priorities. He would deal with that problem later.

Ezra asked Toby and Zeeney to go to Anna May and ask her to supply food for four days. If she protested, they would simply have to remind her that it was for the new boatyard that Mr. Pooles had ordered the three boys to complete. Ezra was sure that by now Anna May had heard about this project. Nothing stayed a secret long on this plantation that would escape Anna May's knowledge. Yes, she did know about the boatyard, but wondered why they wanted so much food, and the type of food they requested! Anna May shook her head at the boys.

"Salt pork, nuts, berries, beans, and even pemmican. Why do you boys want dat awful stuff?"

"You jus' come here an I feed you some real good home cooking!"

Toby and Zeeney explained to Anna May that they had fallen behind on the project Mr. Pooles had assigned them and that the only way they could finish on time was to stay there day and night. They would eat as they worked. Since there was no way to store the food they would need, it had to be non-perishable.

"But pemmican? Why do you want dat stuff? Do you know what it is? Dried Buffalo meat! Toby and Zeeney actually liked pemmican and were not bothered by the description.

"You boys come back here tomorrow, I have all dat nasty stuff ready for you.

They left, mission accomplished!

Ezra's job was to locate vessels large enough to store potable water, as he did not know if fresh water would be available. What he did know was that the boys could not drink the brackish Chesapeake Bay water as it would make them violently ill. He knew this because, as a younger child, he drank the water while playing at the Eastern Beach. He had not wanted to take playing time away while he walked to the well to quench his thirst. The easier and faster way was to drink the nearby bay water. He could still remember the pain and knew that falling ill on their adventure would have a catastrophic effect. The jugs had to be large enough to hold enough water for four days, but compact enough to fit in the limited space on 'Deception.'

He found some tin vessels that would work, but they had no lids. He finally decided that leather pieces, large enough to cover the tops would work. He would fill each, and then tie off each top with the left over leather strapping that Toby had obtained from the tanner. Ezra would fill and seal the cans the day before the adventure started to assure that the water would not turn bad on them. He did not know for sure, but assumed that, if stored properly, well water should stay drinkable for several days. He would just have to take a chance.

It was now Thursday the 14th. The plan was to gather everything they would need at the creek bed the day before the adventure was to start. All the supplies they would need would be temporarily stored in the shed and then transferred to 'Deception' early on the morning of the 16th. They would not waste the night before by staying over at the creek bed; those nights were allotted to the adventure. They would arrive as early as they could that morning to get a good start on this very important day. They had no idea how far or where they would end up the first night. It was unanimously agreed that they would head east, toward the Chesapeake and away from Baltimore town. They also agreed that Zeeney would be, at least for the beginning of the adventure, the captain of 'Deception.' He had repeatedly handled the boat the best during the sea trials. Ezra would be the first mate and poor Toby would be the crew. He just could not figure out that rudder.

Friday, July 15th arrived and the boys gathered late in the morning with all their goods. Ezra had his water jugs in his trusty satchel, being careful not to spill any of the water he had drawn from the well. He had sealed the cans with the leather tops and leather straps, but had tested and found that the cans were not watertight. If turned on their sides, the water would slowly leak out. It was too late to come up with another plan so he showed Toby and Zeeney and explained the cans' deficiencies. They would just have to be careful. The leather tops were not very functional, but they would keep debris from entering. Toby and Zeeney showed Ezra the food Anna May had prepared for them. Wrapped in a linen material were five different packages of food. As the boys unwrapped the linen bundles, they revealed the requested food. Laying before the boys was salt pork, berries and nuts of different types, dried beans, and of course, the pemmican. Ezra admitted that he had never tried pemmican, but knew they were limited in their selection.

Toby and Zeeney both said, "It's real good! We eat it all the time!"

There in the shed were all the items they guessed they would need for the next day's big adventure. They had the food, water, the makeshift tent that was left over from the sails, flints, more rope, some blankets, changes of clothes, and even a cook pot. The boys had no idea if they would cook anything, but would if they had the chance and could come up with ingredients to complement their simple foods.

As they stared at the pile of supplies, they wondered, "is this all going to fit?"

Chapter 32

J uly 16, 1746. No other day in their lives had had the significance of this day. The adventure of their lives was about to begin. None of the boys could sleep. Toby and Zeeney left their homes even earlier than usual, but when they arrived at the creek bed Ezra was already loading 'Deception.'

"I'm always waiting for you two," joked Ezra.

Toby and Zeeney could only laugh, but started to load the boat anyway. It was pretty well packed. There was still room for the boys, but not much. The bulk of their items was stored amidships under the outrigger supports, with the remainder stored in the bow. This would allow just enough room for Ezra behind the headsail mast, Toby, just forward of the aft sail mast, and Zeeney, at the tiller.

The sun had barely shown itself, but that did not deter this group of adventurers. They wanted to get on the water as soon as they could. They had no idea of what the day would bring. Before that day they had only sailed on Bear Creek and slightly out onto the Patapsco River, but always within sight of Bear Creek. After today, and in the coming days, they would be in places they had never dreamed of. In their entire lives none of the boys had ever ventured more than two miles from were they lived. Who knew how far they would go and what they would experience! They were excited and frightened at the same time, but none of them mentioned this to the others.

When 'Deception' was ready, Captain Zeeney said, "My brothers, we have done things that none of us thought we were capable of. Today we start the greatest adventure of our lives. May God bless us and guide us carefully to whatever we will discover, and then safely home."

He climbed into the boat and his first mate, Ezra, and crew, Toby, pushed 'Deception' into deeper water. Captain Zeeney inserted the keels, assisted by his crew, aware that they had never come up with a better system to secure the keels, but knowing that it would not be a deterrent to their trip. They could fix this later.

Captain Zeeney's crew pushed 'Deception' toward the wind as the captain raised first the head, then the aft sail and affixed the sheets approximately where he thought a 'beam reach' would be. They drifted the boat away from the wind and as it started to take the boat, they jumped into the crowded space. As they settled in, all of the boys glanced at each other. All they could do was smile; their adventure had begun. When Toby and Ezra looked back at Zeeney, they were surprised that tears streamed down his cheeks Neither of the two boys could understand the pride that Zeeney was experiencing and what this very moment meant in his young life. Zeeney saw the boys staring at him, as he wiped his tears.

"What are you two looking at? We have a boat to sail!"

For the very first time, Captain Zeeney sailed 'Deception' out of Bear Creek, but would not return that day. Tonight their final destination would not be Bear Creek. He thought to himself that he really should know where they would end up that night, after all he was the captain! But he had never been the captain of a boat before, and he had certainly never been on an adventure.

"This has been pretty much of an adventure so far," he thought.

He knew in his mind that, as captain, he had a responsibility to his crew. Zeeney was not foolish; he knew that from the beginning it was

Ezra who really called all the shots and could have easily named himself captain. What were he and Toby to do? Neither one of them had thought anything other than the fact that they were slaves; they were owned by Mr. Pooles and his family, and that made Ezra their master. But Zeeney had known Ezra all his life, and he just did not feel that the idea of master ever entered Ezra's thoughts. To Zeeney, they were friends, they were brothers, and they were equals! These thoughts gave Zeeney a great deal of respect for Ezra.

"Ezra," he thought, could do whatever he pleased with us, but he treats us as brothers. I love Ezra."

When 'Deception' cleared Bear Creek, Zeeney made his first decision as captain. He knew that Ezra had stated that he wanted to head toward the Chesapeake and away from Baltimore Town, and that he would consult both Ezra and Toby before he made any major decisions, but this decision was rather easy. As they left Bear Creek, Zeeney could see, in the distance a point of land directly ahead, but slightly to the left, of where they were sailing. It was very far away and distorted by the haze on the water. To the left of the boat was the shoreline where the dirt road that they had used so many times to transport items to the creek bed was located.

"I can't believe that I am actually looking at the dirt road we walked down so many times," Zeeney thought.

The wind, as usual, was blowing from the south, and they had done their typical 'beam reach' down Bear Creek to the Patapsco. Since Zeeney knew they were headed toward the Chesapeake and he remembered that they had decided to stay close to shore he determined that they should sail 'close hauled' toward the Chesapeake. This would take them farther away from shore than they had ever been. He had no idea how deep the water was in the Patapsco, but because of its vastness compared to Bear Creek, it had to be very deep. He did not want to venture too far from shore, but on the other hand, he did not want to tack incessantly. Zeeney felt that the beginning of their adventure should be fun, similar to what Ezra had done with swimming lessons. He looked at the point in the hazy distance and then back to the shoreline where the dirt road ran. Then he made his plan. They would continue 'close hauled' until they could see an end of land on the left. At that point, they would end their larboard tack, and the captain would order a starboard tack. As Zeeney thought this through, he decided that although this would take them farther from land than they had ever been, the sailing conditions were very favorable and the bay was fairly calm. They would be safe. They continued on this course for about an hour. As they sailed, Captain Zeeney discussed his plan with his crew.

"We will sail 'close hauled' until we see the land bend to the left, where Eastern Beach is. When there is enough space to move, we will tack to starboard."

Everyone onboard knew from Ezra's lessons that the direction of tack was determined by where the wind came from, if from the right, starboard, and from the left, larboard. Since they were moving from right to left it seemed confusing, especially to Toby. What they had to remember was which direction the wind came from relative to the boat. That really determined the direction of tack, wind from the right starboard, wind from the left larboard. They continued on their larboard tack for sometime. Captain Zeeney wanted to be sure that they would easily clear the land to the east. He did not want to take his crew through multiple and unnecessary tacks. All of the boys were really enjoying their first sailing experience on an actual trip. It was quite pleasant!

When Captain Zeeney was quite confident that they could make the tack to starboard with room to spare, he ordered the tack. They had all agreed that they would use the terms and signals that Ezra had learned from the sailing book in his father's library. They had not yet experienced a jibe, but knew they would most likely experience one on this trip. While on sea trials, they had agreed to use the preparatory command, "Ready about," from the helmsman, and "Ready," responded by the crew, followed by, "hard alee," from the helmsman, when the tack actually took place. Because they had never jibed, the command they had not yet used , was "prepare to jibe," followed by "jibe ho." All the boys, even Toby, understood that a tack was to bring the bow through the wind, and a jibe was to bring the stern through the wind. They would use these commands regardless of who was at the helm.

Captain Zeeney gave the preparatory command, "Ready about." Ezra and Toby prepared the mainsheets on both the head and aft sails, and when ready, announced, "Ready." Captain Zeeney quickly moved the tiller to the right, which brought 'Deception's' bow through the wind and onto a starboard tack. As soon as both of the sails moved through the force of the wind to the opposite side of the boat, Toby and Ezra cleated their respective mainsheets. 'Deception' was now heading back toward, but parallel to the land on the left. There was plenty of water to their left, therefore another tack would probably not be required for quite some time. Zeeney had already learned how to judge where a tack would take them. By looking at the stern quarter on the leeward, or side away from the wind, he could sight approximately where the next tack would take 'Deception.' He was also aware that he had to compensate for drift, so, whenever possible, he would allow a little more space before each tack.

It was an absolutely beautiful day on the bay. They could not have asked for more. All the boys had remembered to bring hats with large rims, even though Ezra was the only one with fair skin. Toby and Zeeney were aware of the pain that too much exposure to the sun would bring. It was just easier to notice the effect of the sun on Ezra, the boys also wore shirts with long sleeves, although shorter sleeves would have been more comfortable on such a warm day. They had no idea how to judge wind speed and had not yet encountered any heavy wind, but from living on the water all their lives they knew that they would someday experience a much stronger wind. Today the wind was almost perfect for their small craft. The outriggers really seemed to be doing the job; 'Deception' leaned away from the wind, but only ever so slightly. Since the lean was steady, it was very comfortable and easy to adjust to. Zeeney determined that another tack was necessary to larboard, and if they stayed on that tack for a short while it would probably be the last larboard tack of the day as there was a vast amount of water starting to appear to their left.

He gave the command, "Ready about." His crew obediently jumped into action, responding in unison, "Ready." Zeeney then gave the final command, "Hard alee," as he promptly moved the tiller to the left.

"We are getting very good at this," Zeeney thought. He watched diligently as the area of water to their left continued to grow in volume.

"Yes," he thought, "this will be our last larboard tack of the day. We'll head on a starboard tack toward that island off in the distance. There we will beach the boat and camp for the night."

Zeeney had another thought; he hoped the unnamed island they headed for was unoccupied. what if there were hostile Indians there?

As soon as Zeeney knew that they could make that island he would order the last tack of that sailing day. He wanted to make sure he had plenty of space to make the island without being too close to the wind on the final tack. He wanted some comfort room to maneuver and allow for drift, therefore even though they were farther away from land than they had originally planned, Captain Zeeney thought the longer tack to larboard prudent.

After his final call for a starboard tack, he had indeed judged correctly. They were now on a comfortable 'close reach' with room to spare as long as the wind continued from the point on the other side of the Patapsco. Now that the boys were in the middle of open water for the very first time, they were aware of the vastness of the Chesapeake. As they stared toward the horizon, both north and south, except for the land nearby, all they could see was water. They had never before been aware of the size of the body of water on which they had lived for most of their lives. It was enormous!

The final tack to the island in the distance took far longer than any of the boys expected. They had now been at sea, they guessed, three or four hours. Even though they had left very early this morning, they knew, from the angle of the sun above their heads, that noon was probably one to two hours away. They discussed the distance remaining to the unnamed island and agreed that based on the distance they had made so far, it was about two to three hours before they would land at the island. They also agreed that they wanted plenty of time before dusk to secure the boat and make camp for the night. They had no idea what they would encounter on the island ahead.

As they finally approached the island, they discovered that it was actually two small islands that only appeared to be one from a distance. There was a fairly small, and quite beautiful gap between the islands. The two islands had white sandy beaches that faced each other and the water in the gap between appeared to be very shallow and to have the same sandy bottom as the two beaches. As they discussed a plan, it was decided to shoot into this gap and beach 'Deception.' They would camp on the first island that they had seen because it seemed less exposed to the elements than the second smaller island. They further decided to run one of their spare lines from the bow cleats to one of the small trees on the shoreline. Since the gap in between the two islands was both narrow and shallow, they could easily ford it to explore the smaller island.

As planned, Captain Zeeney ordered Toby to drop the aft sail and Ezra to let the headsail mainsheet all the way out so that they would be on a run. When he judged that they had enough inertia to beach in the gap, he would order Ezra to drop the headsail. This was accomplished flawlessly. Anyone watching would have thought that they had been sailors forever.

Chapter 33

As 'Deception' chugged onto the soft sand in the gap between the two small islands, Ezra jumped over the bow as Toby tied the line Ezra was carrying to the bow cleats. Ezra tied his end to a medium sized tree in the wooded area just where the beach ended. He looped the line around the tree several times then finished with a knot. He wanted to make sure that 'Deception' was tied off well so he did not find her gone the next day due to wind or water. He doubled back to the boat to make sure that Toby had securely tied the line to the cleats. Toby had over tied the knots, as was his habit.

Zeeney and Toby were busy offloading their supplies, food, and water onto the beach.

"This is truly a beautiful view," Ezra said. Toby and Zeeney had been preoccupied with their work and did not really notice.

"Yes, it is," they both agreed.

"Where do you think we ought to pitch the tent?" asked Zeeney.

"When I was tying off the boat at that tree, I noticed a clearing just on the other side of the island before you reach the far beach," answered Ezra. "Let's go check it out. If it looks all right, we'll dump all our stuff there and start exploring these islands. It doesn't look like anyone has ever been on them before. What do you think, Toby?"

"I think I'm hungry, that's what I think. Why don't we eat, then explore?" he responded .

"I'm for that, we haven't eaten all day, although I'm not really all that excited about our selection of food," Ezra said. "Let's build a small fire and cook some beans, then we will have the other stuff to go with it."

Ezra was not looking forward to his first experience with pemmican. They gathered some firewood into a pile downwind of where the campsite was to be. They found some kindling in the woods and quickly had a small fire burning. The cook pot that they had brought would be useful, especially for the beans, and possibly they could concoct some sort of stew with the pemmican and salt pork they had brought. They would not eat well, but they would not starve either. Ezra had brought enough water to last until Tuesday at their present rate. As they planned to arrive back at the creek bed on Monday they should be fine. There was enough to drink as well as to cook with as long as they did not use it unwisely. Ezra took it upon himself to monitor its usage. He didn't want to run out. They would not perish of thirst, but it certainly would not be comfortable.

After their late dinner, which would also act as supper that night, he and the boys were anxious to explore. He was not crazy about the pemmican, especially the texture, but Toby and Zeeney acted like it was a treat. They headed directly for the water gap that joined the two islands; they could tell that the island to the north was much smaller than the island they had chosen as a campsite, so they would explore that first. The first thing they noticed about both islands was the trees. They were totally different than where they lived and there were no pine trees at all. The eastern shores of both islands were rocky and they could tell they had been eroded by the constant battering of the Chesapeake. They really liked the gap between the two islands. It was sandy like the beach, and because it was fairly shallow, it only came to their knees at the deepest part. The water was quite a bit warmer than the bay. As they continued around past the rocky eastern shore, they were on the backside of the island, the western side. Like the gap between the two islands, the western shore was sandy, and they could see that the sandy beach continued down the western shore of the island they were approaching. They stood for awhile at the ridge at the end of the small island, peering down the length of the beach. It was quite breathtaking and far more beautiful than the Eastern Beach they had played on as children back at North Point. They discussed this for a while and concluded that these beaches were a result of being on the leeward side of the island, away from the wind, and that they were pristine because men had not come here. Maybe Toby was right, maybe they were the first people ever to land there. They walked down the lovely beach and thought how wonderful it would be to swim off this beach in the summer. If the bottom was the same sand, it would be delightful. They continued on down the beach and then back to the gap. They could see that there were few trees at the north side of the small island, and that the real concentration of larger trees were massed at the southern side of the larger island. When they got back to the gap, instead of heading for it, they forded directly to the other identical beach on the larger island. The water there was just a bit more than waist deep and the boys discovered to their delight that the bottom was an extension of the beach. They would definitely be back here in the summer!

They transversed the larger island the same way, ending back at the campsite. Except for the concentration of larger trees at the southern end and the size of the two islands, they were identical. The boys knew that in the future they would definitely be spending summer days here on these islands. They even discussed the possibility of building a permanent structure, one they would use for extended summer stays. Heck, they built a boat, why not a cabin?

"Another adventure," said Toby with a sigh.

Back at the campsite, dusk was starting to diminish their vision so they pitched the tent and built the fire up. They decided that, although they were not really tired, they should get to sleep early because they wanted to get an early start in the morning. While at the northern end of the small island, they had noticed a much larger island in the distance to the north. This would be their goal the next day and probably as far as they could go on this adventure. Although they judged the distance to the next, larger island to be approximately half the distance they had traveled the first day, they knew that sailing back to the creek bed would be a very long sail so the next island would be their last stop on this trip.

The boys settled into their long, but strangely shaped tent. They were glad they had it, especially if it rained during the night as it appeared it might. The night sky was very threatening. They had just been in the tent a few minutes when the attack happened. They did not realize what it was initially, but first one boy, then all three started slapping themselves. They were being attacked by mosquitoes and the swarm must have been huge! Their tent was sealed fairly well where it touched the ground, but no consideration for a front door flap had been incorporated in the original design. They had thought that what they had would be fine, but they had to stop the onslaught. Although it was a very warm night, there was only one thing they could do, seal the front opening with a blanket they had brought. This sealed the tent completely. It was very warm inside the tent, but now, at least the onslaught diminished and they were able to kill off the mosquitoes that remained by slapping at them. Eventually the boys were able to fall into a restless sleep.

Chapter 34

They woke up early the next morning, all very uncomfortable. It had not been a very pleasant sleep; the ground was hard, and it was hot inside the tent, and of course, there were the mosquitoes. As they struck the tent and started to load the supplies back into 'Deception,' they discussed the miserable night and ways to fix their condition in the future. If, and when, another trip took place, they would have to include some creature comforts for the tent. They knew that the blanket worked, but it did not allow for the circulation of air, and there was a breeze. That is when the boys noticed the strange phenomenon happening. For the very first time, the wind was not coming from the point at the Patapsco's mouth, but rather from the distant land that they could barely make out in the early morning haze. The wind was blowing, not from the prevailing south, but the east! None of the boys knew what to make of this. The sky still looked threatening. They would later discover that an even larger body of water, the Atlantic Ocean, was not all that far across from the land that they saw in the haze, and was the cause of most of the bad weather they would experience. Whenever the wind was out of the east, or worse yet, the northeast, they would be in for at least wet, but also potentially dangerous weather. This was a lesson they had not yet learned.

"Look," Ezra said. "The wind is coming from the east, and it looks like it's going to rain."

They quickly loaded and shoved off. There was no time for breakfast this morning The fire had died completely, and they decide just to eat some nuts and berries. This breakfast, however, would be enjoyed while underway.

At first it was a pleasant sail, between a 'beam and close reach' for most of the way. They were about halfway to their destination when Captain Zeeney noticed a perceptual shift in the wind, more to the northeast. He ordered that both mainsheets be tightened to bring the booms closer amidships. The wind was howling at a rate they had never experienced before as they had never encountered an easterly wind. 'Deception' was handling it well, but was leaning more than they had ever experienced; it was quite uncomfortable. After some thought, Zeeney ordered both boys to ease the mainsheets. This took some pressure off of the sails and reduced the leaning, but only slightly.

"Thank goodness for the outriggers," Zenney thought. "Without them the boat would have surely fallen over.

They were a little more than half way to the island, but conditions were deteriorating It was raining now and the wind continued to increase in speed. Zeeney was not positive, but he believed it had shifted slightly more to the east. It was now approaching northeast. If the wind shifted any more to the east, they would have a difficult time making the island, and the last thing he wanted to do was to tack in these conditions. They were very far from land now and a tack would take them even farther. He was afraid. If something bad were to happen they could not swim that far to land. Yes, Zeeney was starting to get frightened, but he wasn't alone.

"What should we do?" yelled Ezra.

"Pray!" Responded Toby.

The wind was increasing in speed even more, but Zeeney did not think it was shifting anymore. They were now 'closed hauled' but heading directly to the island.

"If this holds we will be all right," he thought, but they were still leaning too much, although they were making good speed. If they were not all so frightened, this could have been their best sail ever.

"Toby, ease your mainsheet completely and then drop the sail we have to take some pressure off."

Toby followed Zeeney's order immediately. 'Deception' seemed to handle the strong wind better now without losing the speed they had enjoyed. Now only several hundred feet from the island, they thought they had a chance; they might make it. Since Zeeney had held the boat to 'close hauled' for most of the harrowing trip, there was room to fall off and make landfall on the lee of the island. The only benefit would be that the island would partially block the now heavy wind and make their approach safer. They could see the waves slapping at the shoreline of their island destination. Relief was starting to circulate throughout the crew.

Zeeney thought, "Just 100 feet more and we're safe."

He guided the boat to the lee of the new island. Because he felt the wind die down as he entered the shelter of the island, he did not order the remaining sail's mainsheet to be eased. He realized that if the island did not block the wind somewhat, they would be larboard, 'close hauled.' He still had the head sail set for 'close hauled' but he did not want to lose speed. He thought that the wind would diminish more as they made their way to the sandy beach on the lee of the island. Unfortunately, Zeeney was wrong. Just twenty feet from landfall, the heavy wind clocked around the back of the island and hit 'Deception' with a vengeance! Even with just the headsail up it was still too much. If the sail would have been eased more they may have faired better, but when the gust hit them, their entire world was turned upside down. 'Deception' had flipped on her side dumping all of the contents inside the boat, including the crew, into the foamy water!

Chapter 35

Mr. Pooles decided that he would take a carriage ride down to the creek bed early that morning before church. The sky was threatening and the wind was picking up from the northeast. Jeremiah was concerned about Ezra and wanted to check on his progress. When he arrived at the creek bed, he was surprised to see no activity at all. He assumed that he would see the three boys scurrying around, trying to catch up on their work schedule, but he saw nothing at all.

"Ezra!" he yelled out, but received no response. He yelled again as he walked across the creek bed. He wondered if they had slept in this morning, but where could they sleep? He saw the tool shed up on the rise and determined that this was the only place they could seek shelter for the night. The mosquitoes this year had been particularly bothersome; there was no way they could sleep out in the open. He headed up the rise past the large debris pile and toward the shed. As he got closer to the shed he noticed, for the first time, the large pine that was laying on the rise, hidden by the debris pile.

"Why would someone have brought this tree down?" Jeremiah wondered. "It has nothing to do with the creek bed clearing."

As he walked along the length of the felled pine, it was evident that much of it was missing. He could see the tree limbs at the far end and about three feet of a trunk stub, but the entire middle of the tree was missing. He would definitely take this up with Ezra as soon as he found the boys. He looked back down at the creek bed. Yes, some clearing had taken place but it did not look all that different than the day he and his men had stopped at the creek bed to check on Ezra before.

"If they are working practically around the clock, why haven't they made more progress?" He thought.

This he would also take up with Ezra as soon as he found him. Jeremiah headed to the shed. As it was the only place Ezra and the boys could be, but curiously, the shed was locked from the outside.

"How could they have done that?" he thought.

This was becoming quite curious. Jeremiah was starting to get very concerned about the well-being of his son as well as Toby and Zeeney. It was unlikely, but Indian raiding parties had been spotted in the area and they would be more than happy to take three young boys and force them into slavery. The Indians had even been known to try to ransom young boys back to their families, especially young white boys.

Jeremiah was now very concerned. He headed back down to the creek. Although he was sure he would have seen them when he arrived by carriage, it was still possible he could have missed them. The shed was locked, so perhaps they were in a different part of the creek bed, around the bend which could not be seen from the creek. They had to be there.

He continued to yell, "Ezra, Ezra!" There was still no response. As he arrived at the creek, he noticed something else that was suspicious. There was a fairly deep trench cut into the creek shoreline. It was about thirty feet long and five feet wide. The trench was filled with water at the same level of the creek and it had obviously been dug by men. Jeremiah continued to yell out Ezra's name, as he walked "I wonder what the purpose of that trench is?" he wondered. When I find him we'll have a real good talk. Please God, let me find Ezra and the two boys. I'll hug them first, I'll berate them second."

Chapter 36

They were all right, wet and scared, but all right. They would have had no way of knowing this, but they were only in about four feet of water, and they could stand on the muddy, mucky bottom. 'Deception' was laying on her larboard side, her sail floating on the water's surface, most of the contents from the boat spilled into the bay, including the entire crew. They were immediately prepared to swim ashore, abandoning 'Deception,' when they discovered they could stand. They urgently tried to salvage anything they could. The food and water were gone. What remained inside the boat was sitting in bay water; they knew it was ruined and immediately looked for what was salvageable. The tent floated on the surface and one of the blankets remained inside the water-filled boat. 'Deception' was still afloat. She had not sunk, but at this point, was nothing more than driftwood. The boys knew immediately that they would have to save her; no one knew they were on this remote island in the middle of the Chesapeake. They now had no food or water and what little they had consumed would not sustain them on this desolate piece of land far from their home. They would never be found and starve to death or die of thirst. They knew that their situation was desperate.

"Feel around on the bottom, see if you can find anything that will help us," Toby yelled.

They started to dive in the murky water and came up with some lengths of rope and another blanket. As they came across other items, like the linens that wrapped the food or the water cans they simply tossed them back in the sea. Suddenly, they were aware of another problem; they weren't stationary. 'Deception,' either by the strong wind or the current, was slowly drifting into deeper water. They had to act fast; they had to save 'Deception!' Without her, they had no hopes for survival. Even with her, their chances were slim. They knew if there was some way to save her, at least they would have a chance. They would return home tired and hungry, but they would return. Toby attached one of the ropes he had found on the bottom to the starboard bow cleat. He noticed there was still one length of rope clinging to the inside of 'Deception,' and Ezra had a length on his shoulder.

"Let's see if we can pull her ashore," yelled Toby.

"It will never work," replied Zeeney. "She's full of water."

"It's worth a try," responded Ezra. "All we have to lose is our lives!"

Holding onto their salvage, the boys started to tug on the boat. They were making little progress; either the wind or the current, or a combination of the two, were stronger than they. They were stopping the drift of the boat, but could not gain on the forces of nature; she was winning!

Zenney looked around to shore for a possible solution. Above the howling sound of the wind and the waves crashing on the south shore of the island, he yelled out, "Remember when Toby fell in the well? We saved him by using the trees for leverage, maybe we can do the same with 'Deception.' We can join these ropes together and hopefully they'll reach the tree line."

"It's worth a try, let's do it!" yelled Toby.

As Toby and Ezra struggled to keep 'Deception' from being taken by the sea, Zeeney attached the two lengths of rope to one another. He splashed through the shallow water and onto the beach, feeling relieved to be on dry land. He knew, however, that they were still not out of danger. As he ran up the beach and toward the tree line, he let the two ropes play out. The end of the rope slipped through his hands. The two ropes were five feet too short to reach the nearest tree, but they might as well have been fifty feet short. Even if he was able to reach a tree, he would need at least an additional five feet to secure the rope. He realized that 'Deception' was quite a bit heavier than Toby, although they were dragging her and not lifting. Just the same, it seemed to be an impossible task. He stood on the beach in frustration; Toby and Ezra were still hanging on half-way between the boat and Zeeney. Zeeney realized that sooner or later fatigue and the forces of nature would win and they would lose 'Deception.' Somehow, he could not let that happen. He thought somemore about the forces controlling their situation perhaps the large sail laying out on the water's surface was creating drag and making their salvage efforts more difficult. He slowly made his way back toward Toby and Ezra. He could tell that they were reaching the point of exhaustion.

"I think the sail is adding to our problems. If you two can hold on, I'll try to lower the sail and strap it to the boat some way."

"We'll give it our best!" responded Toby and Ezra.

Zeeney reached 'Deception.' He was now in water up to his neck, obviously she was slipping into deeper water; he had to work quickly. Luckily, the cleat for the halyard was on the starboard side and therefore, on the side facing away from the water! As he released the halyard, a thought came to him. "This halyard will be shorter when I lower the sail, but after I lower it I can cleat it off and tie the aft sail halyard to it to lengthen the rope we need to save her. This just might work."

After releasing the halyard, he worked his way up the mast to the top. He could no longer touch bottom. He was not swimming as he held onto the mast, but he was thankful for the swimming lessons just the same. Without them he would have been terribly frightened. He knew that if he had to let go of the mast he would not drown.

When he reached the top of the mast, he realized what a struggle he had ahead of him. With 'Deception' now prone, he would not have the benefit of gravity to help get the sail down. He was going to have to use all of his strength just to get the sail back in the boat. Then he realized another problem. With the wind and the currents, he was only adding to Ezra and Toby's efforts. His added bulk was adding more strain on the already exhausted boys, and he knew he had to work fast. He used every bit of strength he had remaining to force the sail back toward the boom. There was no way to secure the sail to the boat, he was reserving both halyards to lengthen the rope they would need on shore.

Suddenly, Zeeney remembered the strap that held the rudder in place, as well as the strap that secured the keel that was exposed in the starboard outrigger. He would just have to remove one keel and take it to shore with him. He moved quickly to the rear of the boat and released the strap from the rudder. He placed the rudder inside the boat, keeping an eye on it so it did not drift away. He then untied the keel strap and removed the keel, laying it on top of the rudder. He reached over to the top of the boat and to the boom and threw the straps over the sail. He had to dig around under the sail to find the other end, but once he had retrieved both ends, he tied them loosely together to hold the sail to the boom. He looked at the halyards, but could not figure a way to hook them together, so he decided to abandon the headsail halyard altogether. He grabbed the aft halyard which he cleated at the mast; he could use this. At the last second, he decided that he would use the headsail halyard after all. He would tie it to the aft halyard to form a yoke, this way the boat would be pulled evenly and not stern first. He was almost done! Just as he tied the last knot, he saw the rudder and keel slip from the boat. He would have to use his swimming skills to retrieve them. This was easily done, and since the keel and rudder floated, he used them to help him swim. Zeeney could now touch ground and he was relieved. He moved back toward the totally exhausted boys holding the long halyard in his free hand.

"What were you doing all that time?" asked Toby.

Zeeney did not respond.

"If you can hold on just a little longer, I have a plan," Zeeney said. Toby and Ezra liked this, and faint smiles crossed their faces. Zeeney's plans almost always worked and they hoped this one would too!

"I need to take this ashore and place them somewhere safe," Zeeney told them, pointing to the rudder and keel. "Once I return, you and Toby can hold this rope instead. I'll return to the boat and release the one you have been holding and attach it to the end of the halyards. Hopefully, then we'll have enough length to reach the trees."

He ran far enough onto the beach to secure the rudder and keel in a safe place. He was still holding the halyard in his free hand as he turned quickly and raced back to his exhausted crew members.

"Here grab this instead," he handed the loose halyard to Toby and Ezra. They carefully transferred their hands from the line that was cleated to the bow to the new line Zeeney had made. Zeeney waded back to the boat and released the line from the bow cleat then back to where the boys were. He grabbed the loose end of the halyards and securely tied it. This added length seemed to be enough.

Once more Zeeney ran to the beach, but this time he was sure he had sufficient length to reach the trees. He could not wait to tie the longer line to a tree to relieve his two friends. As he had done at the well, he wrapped the line around the first large tree he could find, pulling the line taught, then wrapped the additional length around not one, but three more smaller trees nearby.

With enormous relief, Zeeney screamed as loud as he could, "The line is secured!"

He glanced over and saw Toby and Ezra collapse into the shallow water. Zeeney figured the boys need a break. He was not sure how long they had held the boat, but it was far longer than they should have endured. Zeeney was exhausted as well but he knew that his exhaustion could not be compared to what Toby and Ezra had gone through. As he approached the boys in the shallow water, Ezra slightly in front of Toby, both had their heads hanging down almost touching the water. Zeeney could see that they were both breathing heavily, neither acknowledged Zeeney or looked up. He stood next to them and decided to just leave the boys to themselves. They needed time to recover before going to the next step of the salvage.

'Deception' was now holding her own, apparently not having moved at all since Zeeney secured the halyard lines to the trees. They may be able to save 'Deception' after all. Ezra and Toby made their way to the beach, only to collapse again. Zeeney sat with the boys and commended them on what they had accomplished in the short time at the new island. He was trying to make light of their situation.

"Hey, we didn't get here pretty, but at least where here and we're all safe. I have an idea. While you two catch your breath, I'll pitch the tent and hang the blankets out to dry. The rain has stopped and the blankets and tent will dry in no time in this wind."

When Zeeney mentioned that the rain had stopped, Toby and Ezra looked up. With everything going on neither of them were aware that it was no longer raining.

As Toby and Ezra rested, Zeeney took it upon himself to pitch the tent and hang the soaked blankets on tree limbs. Their food and water were gone, but they would at least have a dry place to sleep that night and retire from the wind. Zeeney did not mind doing this by himself at all. After what the other two boys had done, this would be a pleasure. Zeeney was very tired as well, but he would not admit it to the others boys. He just made idle chatter, trying to take their minds off of the catastrophe that had occurred. He really wanted to try to pull 'Deception' to shore, but did not mention it. He knew that Ezra and Toby would eventually suggest that they try to pull the boat in. He would not have to wait long.

Toby stood up, looked down at Ezra and said, "What say we pull our boat to shore and secure it for the night."

Ezra jumped up and said, "All right, I'm game."

Since this was Zeeney's contraption as usual, they would let him pull from the tree line while they pulled from the beach. They all thought this was going to be terribly difficult, but they were wrong. With the first tug, 'Deception' righted herself and, now floating, was fairly easy to pull. Zeeney's contraption, as they called it, had saved Ezra and Toby from holding the boat, but was totally unnecessary now. 'Deception' glided easily to shore until the remaining keel dug into the bottom. Zeeney took the slack out of the line and tied it to the last tree he had wrapped. Toby ran the short distance out to the boat and loosened the strap that secured the remaining keel. After he removed the keel itself, it continued to glide toward shore with only Ezra pulling. The relief that all the boys felt overcame them. They had saved 'Deception,' as well as themselves, and they would be able to sail home.

The rest of the evening was uneventful for the boys, which they gladly welcomed. They were terribly hungry and thirsty. These boys did not miss many meals and were unaccustomed to this feeling, as well as that of thirst. They could not run to Anna May's cookhouse to see what was in the stewpot. They would just have to endure the night and try to find something the next day. Originally, their master plan was to explore the new island that afternoon and evening, and leave for home early the next morning. They had not anticipated what had happened to them earlier today, which had occupied all of their time. They would have to change their plan, they could not just leave without exploring the island. They would spend Monday exploring and hopefully, finding some food. Tuesday morning they would leave as early as was possible, and as they learned from their experience, weather permitting. They just hoped that their extended absence from the creek bed had not been discovered by anyone.

What a miserable night! Fortunately, the mosquitoes didn't return, possibly because of the bad weather and high winds, or as Toby pondered, they had gotten enough of their blood the night before. They slept fitfully through the night and when they awoke Monday they were terribly hungry and thirsty. They could not cook; they had nothing to make a fire with, and even if they did, they had nothing to cook. They decided that their first exploration of the island would be for anything they could eat; they wouldn't be picky. They had already resolved themselves to their thirst; they would not find water on this small island, but possibly berries. They thought that if they could eat enough berries, they may not be thirsty.

They decided to cut directly through the island to the windward side; the possibilities of food anywhere on the beach were remote. They headed on to the other side without encountering anything but brush, nothing edible. The plan of action they decided on was to crisscross the island from windward to leeward side. Each pass revealed nothing until they were where they thought was about the center of the island. First

Toby, and then the other boys realized they were walking in very wet ground. They thought this was unusual as they were on land as far from the bay as they could be. As they pushed further through the brush, they saw a small stream flowing back toward the leeward side of the island that they would have discovered had they walked up the beach on that side of the island. Ezra walked over to the source of the small spring. Although the entire area was wet, one place seemed to be where the water emanated from the ground. He reach down to where the water was bubbling from the ground and scooped some up with his cupped hand.

"It's fresh, and very sweet!" Ezra stated.

The other boys followed suit. They each took turns scooping water into their mouths. They could not seem to get enough, and it tasted so good.

"We should have saved one of the water cans after all," Toby said. "Maybe they are still in the spot where 'Deception' sank yesterday. We ought to try going back in the water when we get back to the beach. We'll need some water for our return trip, now that we found some to save."

That was their plan. After slaking their thirst, the boys headed back to the leeward beach to get their bearings. They wanted easy access to the spring they had found if they were successful in recovering water cans from the sight of the sinking.

Back on the beach they looked south and realized they were only about 200 yards from their campsite. They also took note of a tree in the tree line that curved outward toward the water, there on the beach. They would use the tree as a landmark when they returned for more water, with or without the cans. They reentered the wooded area and this time, instead of heading directly back to the spring, they took a diagonal course back to the windward beach. Crisscrossing the island, they felt, was the best way to explore, but now the only goal of their exploration was food. Their thirst had been satisfied which helped greatly, but now they were all greatly aware of the gnawing hunger. They had not eaten for two days.

Their first transverse of the island revealed nothing, nor did the second or third. The island was longer by three times than it was wide; therefore, none of their diagonal trips took very long. On their fourth transverse, they determined they had covered about one third of the island without any success, and this worried them. They were just about at the end of the fourth trip across the island when they notice bushes, about twenty yards from the windward beach. These bushes were not unusual except for the fact that honeybees seemed to take a great interest in them. The boys circled to the right to avoid the bees, and found themselves back on the beach. They walked south about ten yards and noticed that there was an indentation in the tree line where these bushes were. They also discovered the reason for the honeybees interest; the bushes were full of blackberries!

"Well great," said Zeeney, "now we found food and we can't even get to it."

"Yeah," Toby agreed, "as hungry as I am, I don't want to be stung by no bees!"

Ezra chimed in, "You know, honeybees aren't real aggressive. They are not like wasps or yellow jackets. If you just swat at them they stay away, and look, there are more of them on the sunny side of the bush. We can go to the shady area and I'll swat while you two pick."

"Grab some of the large leaves on that tree over there," Ezra pointed to a bush-like tree not far away, "and we can use the leaves to store the berries."

Toby plucked the leaves off the bush while Ezra headed to the sunny side and Zeeney to the shady side. Zeeney immediately started to pick, followed by Toby, but they were so hungry that they were eating more berries at first than they were placing on the leaves. Zeeney became aware that since Ezra was swatting and not picking, Toby and Zeeney were enjoying the delicious berries.

"Let's stop eating and pick some for Ezra, he hasn't had any," he said to Toby. They both placed a small pile of berries on the leaves and presented them to Ezra. He accepted them gladly and moved away from the sunny area to devour them. They now had a source of food and water. Normally, if they were back at North Point, they might stop at a berry bush to taste some, but they had never considered satisfying their hunger with blackberries. Today was different, and to them this was one of the most delicious foods they had ever tasted.

Their thirst and hunger now satisfied, they felt they could properly explore the island. They knew that they would revisit both the spring and the blackberry bush later in the day, but they still had to try to salvage the water cans if the current had not taken them away. Now they could explore. Since they were on the windward side of the island, they decided to stay there for a while. They noticed that the early morning breeze was in its proper southerly direction and that yesterday's ominous clouds had been replaced by puffy fair weather clouds. The clouds were backed by an extremely clear blue sky. There was no haze today. They were on the eastern beach of the island; therefore they could really enjoy the beautiful sunshine as the sun slowly rose. Walking north on the pristine beach, they noticed that the beach indented back toward the west, forming a perfect little lagoon.

"I bet this would be a really good place to swim," Ezra stated.

"Didn't you get enough swimming in yesterday?" asked Toby.

"Well, yes," responded Ezra, 'but if we ever do come back here again and are able to spend any fun time, this looks like a wonderful place to swim. All we have done on this trip, in fact, all we have done this spring is work, I want to have some fun!"

"Ezra is right, all we have done is work," Toby and Zeeney both thought.

"Well," Zeeney stated, "if we come back here this summer, let's try to stay three days and devote at least two of them to fun."

The thought was unanimous!

Just on the other side and north of the swimming lagoon the tree line seemed to stop. The rest of the island from that point on was a fairly flat plain interrupted occasionally by scrub bushes.

"You know what? This island would be a terrific place to live," announced Ezra.

"Who would want to live here?" asked Toby.

"I would," responded Ezra. "It has everything, it's fairly flat so the wooded area could be cleared for crops, there is a natural spring that could be easily tapped as a water source, and this plane would be perfect for a house."

Ezra continued. "It's close enough to the mainland as not to be terribly isolated, but yet protected on all sides from intrusion by outsiders. Yes, I could live here and one day I will!"

They cut across the plane and back toward the western beach. As they walked, Ezra pointed out where all the buildings on the property would be located.

"My house will be here to receive the morning sun," he pointed to an area to the right of them. "Over to the left will be the cookhouse, that way it will be downwind of the main house. The work sheds will all be located down there next to the planting fields and the fields will be near the spring."

As Ezra continued, Toby thought, "What is he seeing? That dunk in the water yesterday must have rattled his brain."

"And," Ezra continued, "your two houses will be over here, facing mine, but with back porches facing the western beach, that way you can sit on your porch swings and enjoy the sun as it sets in the west."

"What are you talking about?" asked Zeeney. "We two ain't never gonna own no houses!"

"Sure you are! You two are going to live here on this island with me and my family, in fact, you are going to raise your families here and help me work the land, but as free men."

Both Toby and Zeeney fell to the ground laughing.

"You did spend too much time in the water, laughed Toby. "I think your brain is waterlogged."

"Yes, free men," Zeeney chuckled. "That's going to happen."

"Well," Ezra stated very seriously, "this has always been my dream, almost as long as I have known you two. I knew that some day I would ask my father for your freedom and we could continue our adventures together, but as equals and as men. I just didn't know where this would take place, until today! I will have Father buy me this property and we will all live and work this land."

The laughter continued as they walked to the western beach, but not from Ezra. He was completely serious and dedicated to this goal.

Chapter 37

Jeremiah rushed back to the plantation house and called for his men to gather in front of the porch. He had an announcement to make. His young son, Ezra, and the two boys assigned to work with him at the creek bed were missing. He saw no signs of foul play at the site, but did see some confusing and disturbing things that he would explain later.

"Men, I know today being Sunday is your only day off, but I hope you will join me in the search for these three boys. I would like to organize the search and leave immediately. I hope that some of you men who have good tracking skills will join the group."

What else would they do? Even if the men disliked Mr.Pooles, which none did, they would be pleased and feel a special obligation to join him. Every man intended to be a member of the search team.

Mr. Pooles continued, "Men, those of you who can join me, please meet at the creek bed in one hour. Please be prepared to be away for an extended time. Bring food, water, and whatever you will need to sustain yourself."

With that Mr. Pooles walked through the front door of the house to prepare himself and to inform and console Emily.

One hour later Jeremiah arrived at the creek bed. He arrived at the location of the future boatyard and was relieved and gratified that every man he had addressed from his front porch was in attendance and was apparently prepared to search for the boys.

"Thank you, men. I truly appreciate your efforts and will find a way, some day, to repay all of you. I was here earlier this morning and discovered the boys missing. As I mentioned earlier I could find no signs of foul play, which is very confusing. The shed, where I believed the boys slept at night is empty, but locked from the outside. If the boys were taken, their captors would have most likely not bothered to take the time to lock the door."

"Up on the rise," Jeremiah pointed in that direction, "near the large debris pile is a felled pine tree with a large portion missing. Down at the creek," he pointed in the other direction, "is a large trench cut into the shoreline. I don't know what these things mean, or if they have anything to do with the disappearance of the boys, but I wanted you all to know about them. These strange things had nothing do with the jobs I had assigned to Ezra and his crew, but I wanted you all to be aware of them in case they do have a bearing on their disappearance. We will use this creek bed as the center of our search. We should spread out in all directions and report back here in three hour intervals. If anyone discovers anything even slightly suspicious, please fire your weapons in a volley of two, and continue to do that every five minutes until the search party can converge on your location."

Chapter 38

The three boys were on the large plane that would someday be their homes. Toby and Zeeney were still laughing and poking fun at Ezra.

"Yeah," Toby said," I'm on the porch swing of my beautiful mansion right now. He pretended to swing."

"Yeah, and I'm sitting on my porch of my mansion staring at the sunset. I'm a free man, doing whatever I please," added Zeeney.

But Ezra was not smiling or laughing. He had a very serious look on his face. Zeeney looked at Ezra, and even his demeanor changed.

"You were serious, weren't you, Ezra?

"Yes, I am," replied Ezra.

"Well, how are you going to pull this miracle off?" asked Toby, as his laughing and smiles diminished.

"Well," Ezra continued, "a while back, I overheard a conversation Father had with my two older brothers, a conversation I am sure I wasn't intended to hear. Father told Jake and Samuel, my two oldest brothers, that when they turned eighteen years old he would buy them property to start their own families. Jake was especially excited about this because he is to turn eighteen this fall. He asked father if they would be allowed to take any slaves with them. Father said yes. Samuel, who is sixteen said he did not like that idea because he did not like or believe in slavery, all men should be free. To that Father told both the boys something I found astonishing as well, that he did not like the idea of slavery as well, but found it a necessary evil required to run the plantation. He also said that if he were sure that the slaves wouldn't all run off if he freed them, he might consider freeing them all. Any of the slaves assigned to the boys could be freed by them when they turned eighteen and received their property, but neither of the boys could come back to him for more slaves should the freed ones run off.

For the very first time in either of their lives, Toby and Zeeney walked down the pristine beach and did not say a word. Neither of them ever considered the concept of freedom, it was beyond their comprehension. All they had ever known was slavery, they could not remember being free at all. They were simply too young when they were initially captured.

"Free," said Zeeney.

"Free," replied Toby.

They would have to think more about this; the concept was just too new. Ezra changed the subject.

"Let's wade into the water where 'Deception' almost sank yesterday and see if we can find any water cans."

The boys took off in a run down the beach and then splashed into the water near the campsite. They fanned out over the area and it was sometime before Toby discovered the debris field.

"Ouch," he said as his bare foot stepped on something under the surface. It did not actually hurt him, but he was startled when he stepped on what he discovered was one of the water cans.

In all they found three cans, but no leather covers. This would be all they needed for the trip back. They would head back to the spring and have more to drink for that afternoon, then on Tuesday morning at first light, they would fetch water for their trip home. They would have to be very careful not to spill the water cans because they had no lids, and they would fresh pick the berries so that they would last the trip home. They could only carry a limited amount of water which could easily spill. They would have to be very careful and they would have to ration the water so it would last.

As they walked toward the spring, Toby and Zeeney could only think of one thing, freedom! If Ezra was right about these things, this wonderful island might be their home someday where they would live as free men. Neither of them had ever thought or dreamt about the future. Now they both had dreams!

Chapter 39

The group of men broke up into separate parties, each group with an assigned tracker. There were four groups all together, one for each major direction on the compass: north, south, east, and west. Mr. Pooles initially wanted to go with one of the groups, but at the last moment stated that he would stay and command the creek bed. He would have runners stay in touch with the various groups to relay information back to him as he waited for their signal that something had been found. While he waited, he would investigate the area. He had hoped his suspicion was right, that they had not fallen prey to foul play. He had based this on the shed being locked. What kind of kidnapper would lock the shed behind them? But he could not fathom what the missing part of the pine tree and large trench meant. Something was amiss, that was for sure. Where were those boys? If someone had not abducted them, where in the world could they be?

It was now late afternoon. Jeremiah decided that they would search the area of his property, which was immense, until dark; at that time they would suspend the search and reconvene in the morning. Hopefully they would find the boys soon and they could get back to their tasks of maintaining the plantation. As Jeremiah searched the creek bed for clues, none came forward; the runners that reported back to him on a regular basis offered no news. At eight o'clock, with light failing, Jeremiah called off the search for the day.

They had prearranged a signal of four musket volleys to announce the end of that days search. They would resume at first light the next morning.

Chapter 40

Very early on Tuesday morning, the boys awoke, still not used to the strange surroundings. They had planned that two of the boys, Ezra and Toby, would fetch the water and fresh berries while Zeeney struck the tent and started to reload 'Deception.' They had no idea how long the sail back home would take, and they all prayed for favorable winds and good weather. They wanted to get safely home as fast as 'Deception' was capable of taking them. They were all homesick, but none would admit it to the others. They just went through the paces that would get them quickly underway.

As soon as they shoved off from their future home, Zeeney did a quick analysis of the position of the wind and determined that the only fast way to make it back was to sail behind the two islands they had landed on two days before. They had arrived with those islands on their eastern side, but to go back exactly the same way would mean sailing directly into the southerly wind. This they realized was impossible. If they went to the east, 'closed hauled' to the southerly wind on a starboard tack, they would take forever and might not arrive back in Bear Creek before nightfall. They had never sailed at night and after their harrowing experience, did not want to attempt it. Then, as Zeeney planned, they would go on a larboard tack, sailing behind the two islands and then complete a much shorter starboard tack to the Patapsco. Except for that final starboard tack, they would be close to land. They had decided that after the capsizing of 'Deception,' they would go back to their original plan; "whenever possible, stay close to shore." They fully realized how lucky they had been when 'Deception' went over. Had they been only a few feet to larboard when it happened, the outcome could have been very different. They might not even be making these decisions right now. They could all be fish food!

This day was as beautiful as Monday had been and since they were cutting behind the two islands, the sail was extremely easy. They were not exactly sure how hard the tack on the other side of the island would be. As they recalled there was not a lot of space between the larger island and the mainland; they just hoped there was enough for an easy tack. If they were nose to the wind on that tack, there could be a problem. They decided that it was worth the try; so on they sailed.

When they finally got to the end of the second island, it was obvious that there would be no problem. The tack behind the two islands took them farther east than they realized. By the time they cleared the island, there was plenty of room. In fact, they were on an easy 'reach' all the way to the Patapsco. The sailing gods truly smiled upon them that day. They knew now that it was possible to make it back to Bear Creek by late afternoon, a reach up the Patapsco followed by another up Bear Creek.

Zeeney found the sail back to be much easier than he remembered the sail out. As he rounded the point where Bear Creek converged with the Patapsco he felt greatly relieved; the weather, as well as the wind, had held up. They were almost home. He wondered how boring life would become in the coming days, after all this excitement. He welcomed the change.

As 'Deception' made its way up Bear Creek, the boys noticed in the distance, on the ridge that overlooked Bear Creek, a large dust cloud. They could not yet determine its cause, but watched with fascination as they got closer. They noticed that the dust cloud was actually caused by a sizable group of men on horseback. The boys really did not want to arrive back at the creek bed with all of these men there to witness there arrival, but it was too late now. They could tell that the men had already seen them because the horses stopped. It appeared that the men were all pointing in the direction of the boat. The boys thought that they must be curious about the unusual sight of a small sailboat coming up the creek. As far as the boys knew, none had ever been seen here before. Just then one of the men on horseback did something very strange, he fired his musket in the air, which was quickly followed by another man firing his. Toby, Zeeney, and Ezra did not know what to make of this, but they knew that something was terribly wrong. What followed next made their hearts sink. To the right at the creek bed itself emerged another large group of men on horseback who were racing at an incredible rate of speed toward the group on the ridge. As the boys watched with lumps in their throats, the men on the ridge waved wildly at the new group of horsemen, but continued to point at the boat. The horseman in the creek bed came to an abrupt halt. Ezra glanced over at that group and focused very quickly on one shape, that of his father!

September 1780

Chapter 41

The Marquis de Lafayette was as far forward as he could be on the barge. The 750 men that accompanied him were wearing on his nerves. He did not really understand these new Americans, well poor Americans anyway. He missed the refinement of France, but he was excited by the fight he had found in this new country. It was one he felt might soon take place in his home country; the people of France were growing very weary of the monarchy. He was, for the most part, a man without a country. He had tried to become part of this new country, hoping that the newness of it might give him the excitement for life that he once had. But he missed the language of his home country and longed to revisit it. Living among these near barbarians was very unpleasant to say the least.

His time in Pennsylvania had been very difficult, General Washington had taken an immediate liking to this young Frenchman and had promoted him to Major General in his army. But Washington soon grew tired of Lafayette and wanted him to occupy space elsewhere. It was looking good for the Continentals, as though they might win this war after all. Washington knew that Cornwallis' army had been cornered in Virginia, not far from Washington's home in a place called Yorktown. Lafayette, although ordered south by Washington, saw this as an opportunity to enjoy some of the refinement he missed so much. On his trip south, he had arranged, wherever possible, to live the refined life of his youth and if he could speak his native tongue again, even the better.

Lafayette had discovered that a distant cousin of his had been hired as an executive chef at the Island Plantation of a very wealthy land-owner in Maryland. Letters from his cousin assured him of accommodations unlike any he would find anywhere else in this barbaric country; his employer and benefactor truly lived a European lifestyle. Jacques was truly amazed by this man. Although born in England, his family moved to the Colonies when he was six months old and he was raised his entire life on the shores of this truly remarkable bay. To Jacques the Bay was extraordinary; the people were not, however, no refinement whatsoever. Jacques thought that he would lose his native tongue until he met Mr. Pooles, who was fluent in French. This was remarkable in that Mr Pooles had never left this country since coming from England. He knew that Mr. Pooles had sailed extensively and, to this day, was still an avid sailor. He also knew that he lived a very refined lifestyle on this remote island in the middle of the Chesapeake Bay, so refined, in fact that Mr. Pooles had searched for and found Jacques, a classically trained French chef. He had brought Jacques and his family here on contract to cook just one meal a day for Mr. Pooles and his family. Mr. Pooles made certain that each day all of the ingredients that Jacques required were delivered to the island; fresh meat was slaughtered, fresh vegetables were grown. Best of all, each day the men that worked for Mr. Pooles would bring all the best fresh seafood that Jacques could choose to incorporate into the daily meal or serve as a main course. The seafood in this bay surpassed the best he had ever experienced in France. It was Jacques's dream job. He had a wonderful boss, lived in a truly beautiful place and he was able to enjoy his trade. He also had more than enough time to enjoy his life.

Jacques loved to fish and Mr. Pooles was teaching him to sail. But tonight, he would be able to converse with one of his countrymen, and a relative as well. He would prepare a classic French dinner and they would wile the night away speaking only their native language and speaking of their homeland. His only worry was that Mr. Pooles might demand too much of the General's time and that Jacques would have to take a more distant role. Fortunately, he had convinced Mr. Pooles that, he and the Marquis could become reacquainted for at least the first night since his cousin was visiting for almost a week.

Jacques had personally gone by row boat over to the eastern shore that morning to Worton Creek to catch rockfish, a great delicacy of the bay. After catching two rather large fish, which would be more than enough, Jacques placed them in a large wooden bucket filled with bay water. He wanted to be assured that the rockfish were as fresh as possible when he offered the meal to his cousin.

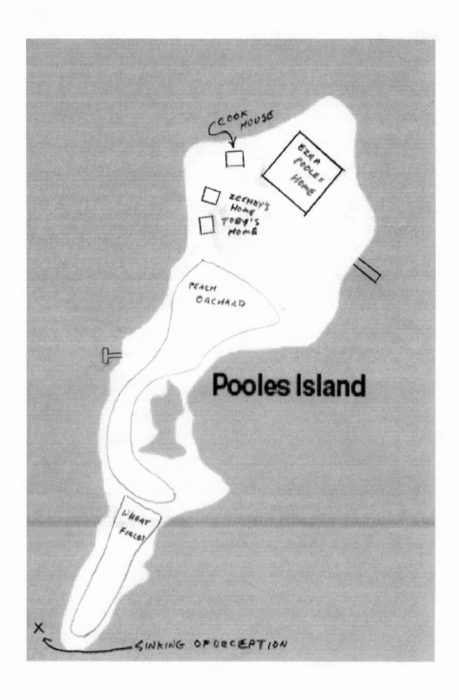

Chapter 42

When the barge finally arrived at Pooles Island, it was moored in a small lagoon just east of the island. The troops on the barge had the option of either taking the short trip to the sandy beach by rowboat or they could swim or wade through the shallow water to the beach. Most chose the latter. Their clothes, equipment, and weapons would be ferried ashore regardless of their choice. The men were to enjoy almost a week of rest and relaxation on this island. They could do whatever they chose: sleep, swim, or eat during the time they were to be there. Then it would be on to Virginia, and back to the war. They would be sure to make the most of their time. The men would camp on the beach in almost luxurious conditions after what they had endured in Pennsylvania. None of the men really minded that their General would be sleeping in the master's plantation goose down bed. They really didn't like the man they all called "the runt" behind his back. If General Washington had picked him to be a general in the army, he could not be all that bad, but most of the men just did not see it that way.

General Lafayette was taken immediately to the northern dock of the island. He had discovered that this island had been named for its first and only owner, Mr. Ezra Pooles, who had built the island into the near paradise it was today. His prosperity, the Marquis was told, came not only from his inheritance, but also his thriving wheat fields and peach orchards. His peaches were especially renowned for their flavor and sweetness and were enjoyed by people as far away as New York City.

As he arrived at the dock by rowboat, the Marquis saw a rather tall and handsome man with graying hair making his way down to greet him. Ezra's outstretched hand acted not only as a greeting, but also as an aid to help Lafayette to the pier. As he shook his hand, Ezra welcomed Lafayette and led him down the short pier to the island. As they walked, Lafayette made note of two sailing vessels docked on the other side of the pier.

"Do you sail Mr. Pooles?"

"Please call me Ezra, everyone on the island, except Mrs. Pooles, calls me Ezra. Why, yes, I do sail as often as my schedule allows."

"Do you sail both boats, or just the larger one?" asked Lafayette.

"Just the larger. I keep that smaller boat for sentimental reasons, although Toby and Zeeney do find time to take her out."

"And who are Toby and Zeeney, may I ask?" replied Lafayette.

"Oh, they are my life long friends. They live on the other side of the island. They help me in running the plantation. Hopefully, you will meet them tomorrow, but first I would like to take you to see your accommodations. I hope they are to your pleasing. Your cousin Jacques is preparing a fabulous Chesapeake feast for you this evening. He would like to get reacquainted with you and requested that the two of you dine alone tonight. Tomorrow night you will dine with my family and me, I have invited Toby and Zeeney and their wives to join us as well."

As Lafayette walked up the extremely wide brick steps that were the entrance to the plantation house, he was very impressed with the quality of what he saw. It was not the largest he had ever visited, but truly one of the finest. Even the brick stairway was unusual in its size and the fact that it formed a half circle that made ascension from any point impressive. What was even more impressive, with the remote location of the island, was how everything in the house, from the furniture to the construction of the house seemed to be the finest of their kind available, Mr. Pooles had certainly gone to great expense to create a luxurious surrounding. Ezra led the General up a very wide staircase to a medium-sized room that was of equal refinement to those he had seen throughout the house.

"I put you in this room because it overlooks the eastern beach. You'll have lovely sunrises to observe while you stay this week and you can also keep an eye on your men who are camping farther down the beach," Ezra pointed toward the eastern-facing window.

"Thank you," replied the General. "This is truly lovely. I will deeply enjoy watching the early sunrise; I would imagine it to be quite beautiful. As to the men, well…"

"Why don't you clean up and rest before supper? Jacques requested that the two of you meet then. He is preparing it, but it will be served by his help staff so that the two of you may reacquaint."

Chapter 43

Buckhorn was in the final stages of preparation. They would launch their canoes and rafts soon, paddle to the south end of the island and land on the beach there. Buckhorn knew from earlier observations that all activity at that end of the island had ceased for the day. The workers had either left on the boat or returned to their homes at the north end of the island. His only concern was that the black men he had seen that lived in the two houses on the north shore would spot Buckhorn and his braves on their way to the south beach. He felt that this was a risk he would have to take. He wanted complete surprise, because with it, casualties on his side would be limited. Even if they were spotted and the inhabitants of the island had time to prepare for the attack, his braves would probably suffer casualties, but he felt there would be few. The forty-eight braves he led far outnumbered the five adult men he had counted while previously scouting the island in preparation for the raid. During the day, there were more men on the island, but the bulk of them had just left on the big sailing vessel. That left just the five he had previously seen. He was not even counting the women and children, in fact, he did not even know what they numbered. Regardless of whether they were seen coming or not, the fate of the people on that island was sealed and Buckhorn and his band of warriors would triumphantly return to the tribe with an abundance of goods acquired from these truly wealthy people.

They paddled away from their shore with a total of eight canoes, four were empty, but being towed, and the eight rafts. On the way to the south shore, the rafts were filled with braves, on the way back later that evening, they would only be loaded with bounty from the island. They would tow the filled rafts back to the mainland, and if they were successful and time allowed, they would return to fill their rafts again.

When they were on the beach, Buckhorn called his braves together.

"My brothers, we must not fail. Kill only the men if possible, but if necessary the women and children. The survival of our tribe requires our success."

They headed out, first through the tree line then the wheat fields, and finally the peach orchard. When they arrived at the end of the peach orchard, Buckhorn gathered his braves again. Everything was going as planned; it was quiet at the plantation house. The attack would commence shortly.

Chapter 44

At the end of their day supervising the workers from Bowleys Quarters, Toby and Zeeney had gone back to their homes as usual. And as usual they decided which porch swing they would sit on and reminisce about the events that landed them on this paradise. As they watched the sun set from Toby's porch swing, they discussed the events of the day, as well as those in the past that were the reason they enjoyed the sunset and the swing from the back porch of Toby's house. Toby's house was situated on the western beach and was next door to Zeeney's, almost exactly where Ezra had pointed that day, over thirty years ago, when he described where their houses would be built.

"Sure is the good life we live," said Toby.

"Yes, it is," replied Zeeney.

"We've been living here for what, thirty years?" asked Toby. "Yes, and its hard to believe the life we have had. Ezra was true to his word. When we came here the first time and Ezra told us that crazy idea he had, hard to believe he really meant this. We're free, we have families and we live the good life."

"That's for sure," said Zeeney, "but do you remember that year back in 46', I gave up all hope of any of Ezra's crazy ideas.

"Yeah, Mr. Pooles was awfully angry when we sailed up Bear Creek and he finally confronted us. As soon as we pulled 'Deception' into that trench we were surrounded by Mr. Pooles men. Most of them were laughing, but Mr. Pooles sure wasn't. He didn't say a word, just grabbed Ezra's shirt and dragged him from 'Deception' we didn't see Ezra again for almost a year. They just sort of left us sitting in 'Deception' as Mr. Pooles left and all his men followed. The next day we didn't know what to do with ourselves, the adventure was over, 'Deception' was built, and the creek bed project was over. We just got up every day and tried to make it through the days that lasted that summer and into the fall and winter. We never saw or heard from Ezra, and surprisingly we never heard from Mr. Pooles. I fully expected to receive some punishment for what we had done, but it never happened."

The following spring of 1747, they finally saw Ezra again. Since they had so much free time on their hands and because they thought that God would bale them out eventually, they started to go to church.

On Sunday, as they sat in the back of the church, Toby nudged Zeeney, "Hey, isn't that Ezra?"

"No," said Zeeney, " he's too big and clean to be Ezra, that can't be Ezra!"

He was wrong.

Outside of the church, Toby and Zeeney stood in the shade of a chestnut tree and waited for the person Toby was sure was Ezra. They saw him leave the church with Mr. Pooles.

Toby said, "See Zeeney, I told you that was Ezra."

Sure enough, the tall good-looking boy that Toby was sure was Ezra headed their way.

"I guess we'll find out now," said Toby.

"Toby, Zeeney, how have you been?"

"See I told you so," Toby exclaimed to Zeeney.

"We've been fine," replied Zeeney. "I bet your life has been hell since your father caught us that day."

"Well," Ezra replied, "not exactly." It was bad at first, but Father soon lost his anger. What did he call my actions? Oh, yes, 'youthful transgressions.' He even said he almost understood what we had done. In fact, he said at my age he might have done something similar, but that adults had to be responsible and act like adults, and that is what is expected of me. Soon after that day Father shipped me off to a private school in Boston. He told me that my problem was that I had too much free time on my hands and that being busy with school would solve that problem. I am to attend this school and then attend a college in the same area. It's called Harvard College. I don't know much about it, but Father tells me I will end up with a decent education."

"Did your father beat you?" asked Toby.

"No, in fact, soon after that day, do you know what Father asked me? Could I teach him to sail? I asked Father about you two and he said he would take no actions against you, that both of you were taking orders from me and you weren't responsible for my actions. Did he leave you alone?"

"Yes," replied the two boys, "but we always wondered why? I guess now we know."

"What ever happened to 'Deception?'" Zeeney asked. "We always wondered about her."

"Believe it or not, she is still in the creek and still in the trench we dug, Father told me, when he was speaking to me again, that the beautiful little boat was too nice to destroy and that when he had time for lessons that would be the boat for me to teach him in."

"Wow!" That was all that Toby and Zeeney could reply Ezra bid goodbye to his two good friends.

"I won't see you for awhile, but I haven't forgotten what I promised you. It will happen some day."

Toby and Zeeney left. They went about their lives and only saw Ezra sporadically during the next five years. It was never as it was the spring and summer of '46, that is until one day in 1752. The boys were summoned to work, in of all places, the creek bed. When they arrived there, they were greatly surprised to find their old friend Ezra alone. He was at the creek and 'Deception' was still in her trench, fully loaded with supplies.

"Hello," said Ezra, "do you remember what I promised you six years ago?"

Toby and Zeeney could only look at each other in total amazement.

"Father has purchased our island for me, and he has assigned you two to help me get it ready to be inhabited. Next week, July 8th, is my birthday and, as of that day, the island is mine. He is also giving me another present. Do you know what that is?"

Toby and Zeeney shook their heads, they were in shock.

"You two, you will belong to me."

"We will be your slaves, Ezra?"

"Yes, as of my birthday July 8th, you two will be my slaves, but you know what happens on July 9th?"

"What?" asked Zeeney.

Ezra replied, "On July 9, 1752, I am granting your freedom and you may go and do what you please. Of course, my dream is that you come to Pooles Island with me as my partners and help me work the island. I can't do it by myself."

"When do we leave?" asked Toby.

"As soon as you say yes to my offer," replied Ezra.

He then heard a resounding, "Yes!"

Chapter 45

Ezra, now almost eighteen, had grown very tall and lanky. He was over six feet tall. Toby and Zeeney still were not sure how old they were, but assumed they were about the same age as Ezra. So whenever Ezra had a birthday, so did they. While not as tall as Ezra, they were nonetheless tall. The three boys didn't fit quite as well in 'Deception' as they did on their famous adventure. Luckily they were not carrying as many provisions. There was no tent or blanket. Toby and Zeeney did not see what appeared to be food stuff, but there were cans that they assumed were water.

Finally Toby asked the question. "Gee, Ezra, how long are we staying on your island?"

Ezra, responded, "I don't know for sure, maybe three or four days, whatever it takes. You two got someplace else to go?"

"No" responded Toby and Zeeney.

"We just noticed that there weren't many provisions, that's all."

"Oh, I guess I should have told you, I've actually been to the island many times before today. Everything we will need is already set up. Captain Zeeney, are we prepared to shove off?"

"Yes, Sir, let's go," responded Zeeney.

He assumed his place at the rudder as Toby and Ezra guided 'Deception' to deeper water. As he had done before, he placed first one, then the other keel in the slot. He noticed that Ezra had never modified the leather strap arrangement and Toby and Ezra automatically started to lash the keels. Although it had been five years since their last adventure, none of the boys, now men, seemed to need a reminder on what to do, it seemed as natural as it had five years earlier.

Zeeney started raising the headsail as Toby and Zeeney guided 'Deception' into the wind, that, as usual, blew from the south. Since they were now seasoned sailors, Zeeney went ahead and raised the aft sail as well, setting the sheets for both sails at approximately 'beam reach.'

Turning the boat away from the wind, the two men in the water jumped in. They were off, down Bear Creek and as far as Toby and Zeeney were concerned, on another adventure. They had no idea what awaited them at Pooles Island, but they were certain that Ezra had a plan. Neither of them said a word or inquired what Ezra had planned. And the idea of freedom was such a new concept that they did not know what to make of it.

Zeeney, from his position at the rudder could see how poorly the men now fit in 'Deception.' This was especially true of Ezra whose long arms and legs dangled up over the rails. There simply was not room for him. Toby faired only slightly better than Ezra, but Zeeney had the luxury of the stern of the boat which had slightly more room, but a lot less than he remembered from five years before.

It was a beautiful day with perfect sailing conditions and apparently they would have an uneventful sail. Although, deep in their minds, they were reminded of the mishap that had befallen them five years ago.

Zeeney was still impressed at how well this boat sailed. They continued their 'beam reach' out of Bear Creek and onto the Patapsco. Zeeney was not at all surprised that the conditions were almost identical to their previous adventure.

He yelled to Ezra, "Are we stopping at the two islands?"

"No, all our provisions are at our island. I thought we would push on and go directly there, that is, unless you want to repeat our trip of five years ago?"

"No thanks, we're all for pushing on," responded Zeeney. "Alright with you Toby?"

"Yes, Sir!"

Zeeney ordered his crew to tighten the main sheets as he guided 'Deception' to 'close hauled' on a larboard tack. This would take them east of the two islands they had spent their first night on some five years ago. But Zeeney decided that they would try to come as close to the east shore of these islands as they could to make their approach to their final destination.

"What did you decide to call your island?" asked Toby.

"I stuck with my original plan and named it "Pooles Island," but it's not my island, it's our Island!"

Toby and Zeeney did not know what to say, so they said nothing. They were moving quite well, with little leaning, a very enjoyable sail. They slipped quickly past the two smaller islands. Toby wasn't sure because Pooles Island was still fairly far in the distance, but he swore he saw another boat near Pooles and it appeared to be at anchor.

"Ezra, do you see that up ahead?" asked Zeeney.

"What's that you see?" replied Ezra.

"I'm not totally sure, but it looks like another bigger boat and it appears to be anchored at our island," responded Zeeney.

Ezra replied, "That can't be, no one is allowed on our island, it's posted. We will just have to check it out when we get there and evict the intruders if necessary."

Toby and Zeeney could not see Ezra's face because he was faced towards the bow, but he had a very huge grin wrapping from ear to ear. Since the sail was so easy and uneventful and they had jibed and were now on a broad reach, Zeeney suggested that they make landfall in the eastern lagoon, where the intruding boat appeared to be anchored. They would sail near the intruder and if they were ashore, ask them to promptly leave.

Toby asked Ezra, "What if the intruders have ill intentions?"

With that Ezra did not answer, he reached to the floor of the boat and retrieved his musket which he waved above his head. Still facing away from Toby and Zeeney, his non-stop grin almost pained him.

They were now more than half way between the two small islands and Pooles Island. The intruder boat was beginning to take shape. They could tell, that the boat at anchor was quite a bit larger than 'Deception' and that it was also a double master. The closer they got revealed that this boat, coincidentally, was almost the same color as 'Deception.'

Ezra finally turned around. it was difficult for him to disguise his grin, but he did a fairly good job.

"Captain, why don't we sail past the intruder to her stern, then jibe past her to determine if anyone is aboard. If they are indeed aboard the vessel they are not intruders, but if they have gone ashore we will definitely have to deal with them."

Again he turned away and waved his musket, the grin returned.

Neither Toby, nor Zeeney knew what to make of this. It had the makings of a bigger adventure than the first; they could be shot or killed.

They continued on and could see the intruder boat quite clearly now, she was beautiful. In fact, although Toby and Zeeney had not seen many boats, it was absolutely breathtaking. The lines were perfect, both masts were raked slightly to the stern, which, even sitting still make the boat look incredibly fast. They were approaching her larboard side, therefore they could not yet see her stern to determine the beam of this interloping boat. From their vantage point, Toby and Zeeney could tell that there appeared to be no one on the boat, unless they were below, and this gave them a sinking feeling. They were probably going to have to confront the intruders and that might become a dangerous situation.

'Deception' was almost to the stern of the intruder and Toby and Zeeney could now see that this boat had a sizeable beam, it appeared to be nearly nine feet wide. They also noticed that like 'Deception,' the name of this unidentified boat, was lettered in gold leaf.

"Looks like 'Deception's' big sister," exclaimed Toby.

They were finally directly behind the intruder. Zeeney was determining when to jibe when Toby spoke out again. "Look, that boat has a name just like our boat, what's that first word Ezra?"

"'Final Deception,' chuckled Ezra, "and look where she is from, Pooles Island, Maryland."

Toby and Zeeney stared in utter amazement, what did this mean? Had someone else claimed this island ahead of Ezra and anchored their beautiful boat near their new island? Ezra could stand no more. As 'Deception' quickly past 'Final Deception,' he turned to Toby and Zeeney without trying to conceal his joy.

He said. "That, gentlemen, is our new boat. I had it built and commissioned in Baltimore town and delivered here weeks ago. I also had the boat builder install a permanent mooring so that the boat would always be safe. Let's go ashore in the lagoon, there is a dinghy beached there that we can row out to 'Final Deception,' I want you two to look her over."

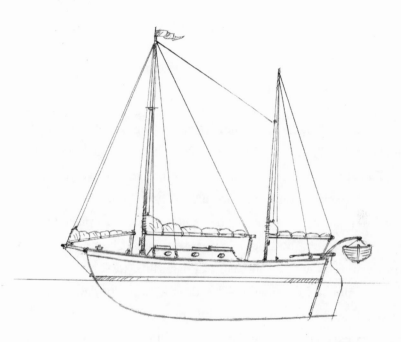

'Final Deception'

Chapter 46

Ezra walked Toby and Zeeney over to the small dinghy that belonged to 'Final Deception.' He had it built by the same boat builder as 'Final Deception' and explained that it added great convenience, but they were not paying attention. Toby and Zeeney kept glancing out at the beautiful boat in the lagoon. They still had a special place in their hearts for 'Deception,' but the new boat was a great fascination. They could not wait to board her and as Ezra had said, "look her over."

Ezra continued to explain. The dinghy was specially built to accompany 'Final Deception.' On the stern of 'Final Deception' is something called davits that raise the dingy out of the water and hold it in place there. That way you can take it with you wherever you go, then you can anchor out or moor like we are doing here and use the dinghy to get to shore.

Toby and Zeeney just shook their heads.

"What a modern age we live in," they both thought.

Ezra continued, "It is a simple, but practical craft and as you can see it is painted the same color as 'Final Deception.'

"Did you see her name?"

"No," responded Toby and Zeeney.

They looked down at the stern of the double ended boat and saw the name "Elizabeth Anne."

"What's that all about?" asked Zeeney.

"I'll tell you later, let's row out to the new boat.."

They pushed the little dinghy into the shallow water and jumped in and since Ezra was familiar with her he rowed. He came around to the stern of 'Final Deception,' and pulled up perpendicular to the stern of the new beauty.

"See those hooks? Fish one through the eyebolt and secure them with the leather straps, once secure we can climb the ladder on the side of the boat."

Zeeney finished first and headed up the ladder, followed by Ezra who was in the middle. Toby, who had been in the stern and had trouble securing the hook, finally finished and, of course, used the famous Toby overdo knot to secure the hook.

Ezra thought, "One of these days I'm going to have to teach him knots."

Once on the bridge, as Ezra referred to it, he reached over and cranked a device that caused the dinghy to raise out of the water. Once in its home position he placed two long rods on "Elizabeth Anne" to secure her in place.

"With this contraption you can take the dinghy anywhere you want to sail even in rough conditions.

The convenience of being able to anchor out or tie up to a mooring was beyond Toby and Zeeney's imagination.

They looked around the extraordinarily beautiful boat, with its polished wood, polished brass, and every conceivable modern rigging device that was available.

"She is thirty two feet long including the bow sprit."

"What's a bow sprit?" asked Zeeney

"It's that thick polished wood that extends from the bow, besides the two racked masts. This boat has a jib, a forward, smaller sail that attaches to the front mast and runs down to the bowsprit, that gives her a lot more sail area. In this area in front of the bridge is a passageway to a saloon, you can get out of weather down below, there are even some gimbaled oil lamps down there to use at night. Her beam is nine feet and it has a full keel that draws six feet, in the bilge are iron ingots to make the boat very stable, and she is!"

"Why don't we head back to shore and get settled for the night. Tomorrow we can take her for a sail and I'll answer all of your questions."

Ezra cranked the "Elizabeth Anne" back to the water and they climbed back in the small dinghy and headed back to shore.

"Remember back when we had our adventure back in 46', I complained that all we did was work?" said Ezra.

"Yes, I remember," replied Toby.

"Me too," exclaimed Zeeney.

"Well, today we settle in, tomorrow, weather permitting, we sail, but for to next two days we play. After that it's all work. We have a lot of work to do planning our future homes."

Chapter 47

Ezra had four tents pitched on the beach, one for himself, one for Toby, and one for Zeeney. The remaining tent, Ezra explained, "was full of everything they would need to plan the future construction of their home. True to his word they just had fun the next two days, they swam in the lovely lagoon with the wonderful sandy bottom and even got a chance to sail "Final Deception." She was not only beautiful, she sailed beautifully as well.

At the end of their third day on Pooles Island, Ezra informed them that they had to finally get back to work the next day, but that this should be very enjoyable work. They would draw up designs for their new homes and they would plan the fields that would be their source of livelihood. They would have to return the next week to North Point Plantation for his family's celebration of his eighteenth birthday, the day that all of Pooles Island would officially become his. He did not have to remind Toby and Zeeney what would happen the next day, although the concept of their future lives was still impossible for them to comprehend.

In the fourth tent, the one no one occupied, were tools and implements to draw up plans for the island. Unlike the primitive and makeshift implements they had used at the creek bed to design and build 'Deception,' here were actual drawing tables, rulers, compasses, dividers, and scribes. Also each table included quill pens of different sizes along with a sufficient supply of inks in various colors. They had certainly come a long way from Bear Creek.

"We will set up north of the lagoon where the plane starts. There we should be able to see the lay of land well enough to draw up plans for new homes. We can't really see the fields because of the trees and brush, but I have maps of the island that we can use to plan the fields. If we can get the homes drawn up before we leave for North Point, I will be very pleased."

The three men started the process of transporting the tables and implements up the lagoon beach to the plane. As Ezra had said, from this vantage point they could easily see over to the western shore of the island. The tree line started just south of the plane, therefore it would be impossible to visualize the future fields. Those would be planned at a later date. They would draw up plans individually and then confer with each other to finish the plans. It was very hard in the beginning, Toby and Zeeney, of course, had never had any formal training in house design. Ezra had had some basic classes at his school in Boston which would help him immensely with this process.

Toby and Zeeney, on the other hand had no idea how to start, so Ezra decided to help them first. He laid out parchment paper on Toby's drawing table and then pinned down the corners.

"Don't worry about making mistakes, there is plenty of paper and ink. Also don't just think in terms of boxed shaped rooms. Think also of round shapes like Father's library back at North Point. Visualize the different components of a house.

"But we lived in one room shacks at North Point, isn't that what we are building?" asked Toby.

"No, of course not," replied Ezra. "You will also have to think as free men with families and houses with multiple rooms."

Zeeney responded, "Ezra, I don't think we even know how to start. Why don't you help us, kind of like you taught us to swim."

"Alright, I already have most of the design for my new home in my mind. Why don't we concentrate on your homes first, I'll show you the basic process and then you can practice and develop the skills you will need to draw the finished homes. One suggestion though, and it is only a suggestion. From the outside your homes should look similar, not exact, but similar. Once the outside dimensions are decided on you can design any interior room layout that you are comfortable with. I will only point out to you rooms that are not functional, or layouts that will be difficult to build. Let me show you some basic designs to give you an idea."

Ezra started to sketch some rough plans. He drew an outline of the outside of a house then some square and rectangular shapes within the outline to represent rooms.

"Pretend that this is a one-floor house and we removed the roof and we are looking through the roof which is removed. This is what it would look like." Ezra used the quill pen as a pointer. "This is a parlor, this is a dining room, maybe this is a library or an office."

"Where do we sleep?" asked Toby.

"Well," continued Ezra," one of these rooms could be your sleeping quarters, or bedroom, but normally you place them on the second floor."

"Second floor, we can have a second floor?" Asked Zeeney.

"Sure," replied Ezra, "just draw another box just like the first floor, but next to it, and don't forget to make room for a staircase from the first floor to the second

"What, no ladder? You mean we even get stairs," Zeeney joked.

"Look, you have the basic idea. Close your eyes and try to see the place you would like to live in and raise a family, then draw it in on the parchment. There is plenty of parchment and, as I said, plenty of ink. Why don't you two work together on the first design then I'll look at it later and offer any suggestions. And don't forget to include a back porch, remember the sunsets."

Ezra headed to his drawing table and let Toby and Zeeney experiment. He looked back and they both stood in front of the drawing table with their eyes closed.

Later that day Ezra took a break from his plans and went over to check on the other two. Next to the drawing table was a fairly large pile of discarded parchment, but Ezra could tell that they were making some progress. For one thing, they were arguing which is always a good sign.

"How are you making out?" Ezra asked.

"Fine, if it wasn't for bonehead here," Zeeney referred to Toby.

"Hey, you don't have to agree on everything. Come up with a basic design then break off to individual tables. Like I said before, your houses should be similar, but not the same. Are you ready to do that?"

"I guess so," said Toby.

"Boy, am I ready," replied Zeeney.

"Let's finish up today and sleep on it. Tomorrow you'll probably have better luck now that you know the basics." said Ezra

"Just like swimming," responded Zeeney.

Chapter 48

The next day, during breakfast, Ezra explained that they only had today and tomorrow to finish, but not to worry. If they had not come up with their plans by then it would not be a problem. He just would like to have them ready for the builder when they returned to North Point in order to give him plenty of time to order the material he would need for construction.

"I should finish my drawings today and can devote all of my time tomorrow to help either of you. How are you doing?"

"Better than we thought," replied Zeeney. "The closing the eyes thing really works.

"How about you, Toby?

"Actually, I think I understand. Why don't we do what you suggested? Tomorrow you can help both of us finalize our plans."

They headed to the drawing tables.

The next day both Toby and Zeeney, working separately, seemed to be making progress. Ezra would take breaks from time to time and glance at their work. He was pleased to see they were actually making very good headway. Their drawings were, as he had suggested similar, but not the same. Both houses showed substantial porches facing the western beach.

Ezra, as he promised, completed his plans and helped Toby and Zeeney. Ezra suggested to both, that the porch encompass the entire

house, not just the back. Now that Toby and Zeeney understood the
process they could appreciate the modifications. Ezra appreciated the
fact that they had completed their plans on schedule. He did not share
this with the other two, but the builder had explained to Ezra that he
wanted the plans as soon as possible in order to have the building
materials they would require delivered this summer. As it was they could
not guaranty completion until the following year. They did not work in
the winter, especially in such a remote location

He also suggested some modifications to their plans, mostly due to
building considerations. Then he showed them his plans, which
impressed them both. It was similar to Ezra's home at North Point, but
obviously represented Ezra's desire for a unique dwelling. After seeing
his plans, Toby and Zeeney asked him why he did not show his house
plans to them in the beginning. It might have made the process easier.

Ezra explained, "I did actually think of that, but then decided that
my plans might unduly affect yours. I really wanted you two to think of
original ideas on your own. Now you have done just that. After seeing
my plans, if you want to make modifications that don't affect the
original design, then you should do just that. We have today to do any
last minute adjustments, tomorrow, we sail for North Point on 'Final
Deception'."

Chapter 49

Friday, their last day on Pooles Island had arrived. Ezra wanted to be back for the weekend to prepare for his birthday the following week and to meet with the builder. He had some other plans that he did not share with the other two. He figured they would find out soon enough. He prepared 'Final Deception' for departure, tying 'Deception' to the mooring to protect her in their absence from the island. Ezra rather sheepishly explained to Zeeney that he hoped that Zeeney would not mind if Ezra was the captain.

Zeeney laughed, "Are you kidding me? You have been so good to Toby and me. You've been like a brother to us most of our lives and have treated us as equals. Next week, you're giving us the greatest gift of all, our freedom, then you're building us houses on this beautiful island and making us your partners. No, you can't be captain, I am!"

Ezra looked strangely at Zeeney.

"Now, I'm kidding," laughed Zeeney. "Except the captain business, I truly meant everything else I said. Just do me a favor, let me captain her sometime."

Ezra smiled, "No problem!"

They released the mooring flag and were off.

Ezra explained, " we will raise both main and aft sails and take her slightly away from the wind, then I'll show you how the jib works. We didn't have one on 'Deception.'

They were off on a beautiful sail on a beautiful boat. Ezra further remarked, that since 'Final Deception' was a much faster boat that 'Deception' due to her longer water line and ability to carry more sails, they had more options and would arrive at Bear Creek much earlier.

The prevailing southerly wind was in place and what Ezra suggested something they had never done before.

"Since 'Final Deception' is so much faster, why don't we sail on a starboard tack towards the eastern shore. That will put us on a nice beam to broad reach all the way back to Bear Creek."

"Sounds like a plan!" said both Toby and Zeeney.

It was truly a fantastic sail. Since none of them had ever experienced any sailing other than 'Deception,' they really did not know what to expect, but this was beyond any of their expectations. They sailed on a very fast starboard tack almost reaching the eastern shore, then Captain Ezra ordered his crew to tack to larboard and set sails for a 'beam reach.' They did it with pleasure.

When they finally reached the mouth of Bear Creek, the Captain ordered a jibe, and asked that his crew drop and store the jib. This gave them control and a very gentle sail up the creek.

As they approached the docks on Bear Creek that had been built after the famous "Adventure" some five years earlier, Toby and Zeeney could see in the distance on the pier what appeared to be a young woman. As they got closer, they could see that she carried a parasol and was very attractive. She was tall and thin and had long light brown hair that was curly, and the closer the boat got to her Toby and Zeeney decided they were wrong, she was, in fact, beautiful. She had a familiar look to her, but they really were not sure why she was here on the pier, or who she was

"Hello, Ezra," she said. "Hello, Toby and Zeeney. What took you so long? I've been waiting here forever."

"She knows us," Toby said.

"How does she know us?" asked Zeeney. "We don't know no pretty white women!"

Ezra luffed the sails and as he drifted towards the pier, Toby and Zeeney jumped from the boat to tie her off.

Ezra jumped from his craft and approached the young woman. Without saying a word, he took her in his arms and kissed her.

"Oh, you're all sweaty," she complained.

Then she said, "Oh, kiss me anyway, I've missed you."

"When did you get in?" asked Ezra.

"The day before yesterday, and I have been dying to see you, what took so long?"

"We had to finish the plans for the house."

"Well, did you?"

"Yes, they are right here in the boat. I'll show them to you at dinner."

"Good, and, nice boat. Am I finally going to get that ride you promised me all those years ago?"

"Yes, next week, after my birthday, I will take you to what will be our future home."

Ezra turned to Toby and Zeeney, "Men, I guess by now you know who this is."

They did but he gave the formal introduction anyway. "This is Elizabeth Anne Thomas, and next year, when our homes are finished, she has agreed to become my wife. Mrs. Elizabeth Thomas Pooles."

Toby and Zeeney now knew why the dingy had been named the Elizabeth Anne, and why Ezra named his new boat 'Final Deception'.

September 1780

Chapter 50

Just as the sun was finally setting in the western sky signaling an end to their day, Toby and Zeeney stood on the porch and bid each other a good night. During the growing season, the sun dictated their bedtime as well as their awakening. As Zeeney was about to leave and turn in for the night, he pointed toward the sunset.

"Do you see that?" he asked Toby. "It looks like men in canoes, lots of them!"

"We better go tell Ezra. This doesn't look good."

They left immediately. They could still run, but not like the day when 'Old Mr. Jim' was chasing them. Around Toby's house and into the field they ran; it was not terribly far to Ezra's plantation house. They struck the metal triangle that was hanging from the porch ceiling which was used to call workers for special announcements. Ezra immediately emerged from the house.

"What's wrong?" he asked, with a look of concern on his face.

"Toby and Zeeney should be in bed by now," Ezra thought.

"We saw many men in canoes paddling toward the southern tip of the island," Toby said.

"How many?" asked Ezra

"I don't know for sure, but a lot, maybe fifty," replied Toby.

"How do you know they were coming to this island?"

"We don't, but why would that many men in canoes head for the open bay at sunset? It just looked suspicious to us. We thought you should know."

"Yes, you were right to come here. It does sound rather strange. Come inside while I come up with a plan."

Ezra did not waste any time. He immediately raced up the wide staircase to the second floor to the bedroom of the General. Ezra knocked and was immediately greeted by Lafayette, who was obviously preparing for supper with his cousin.

"What can I do for you, Ezra?"

"Well, we may have a situation and I would like your help. Toby and Zeeney are downstairs. You will meet them both tomorrow night. Their homes are on the western shore of this island, and every evening before retiring, they sit on the porch and watch the sunset."

"Why is that a situation?" asked the Marquis.

"Well tonight, just before leaving the porch, they saw at least fifty men headed toward the southern beach by canoe."

"How do they know they were coming to this island?" asked Lafayette.

"They don't, but most would be crazy to go across the bay at night by canoe," responded Ezra.

"There is a full moon tonight," stated Lafayette.

"Still crazy," replied Ezra.

"Well, I assume precautions are in order"

General Lafayette, still in his dressing gown, went to the eastern facing window and addressed a sentry posted at the field below the window.

"Soldier!" he yelled. "Go immediately to the encampment and ask Lt. Smithson to assemble the troops with weapons as soon as he can. They are to assemble at the rear of this house and await my orders. I will be down there shortly to instruct the men on what they will do next."

"Yes, Sir, but the men aren't going to like this, Sir."

"They may not like it soldier, but they will do it. Tell them it is a training exercise and that the speed with which they assemble behind the house is of utmost importance."

"Yes, Sir, I'll report to Lt. Smithson immediately and relay your order."

The soldier ran toward the eastern beach.

Lafayette was clearly disturbed by the events that just took place. As he put his dirty uniform back on, he said to Ezra, "Please convey my condolences to my cousin. Perhaps we can dine together another night."

Ezra apologized, "I am sorry, General. Maybe this is a false alarm, but I can assure you that Toby and Zeeney would not come to me if there was not a legitimate reason. I will go back downstairs, arm Toby and Zeeney, and wait for your troops on the front porch."

Ezra left. He felt bad about ruining the General's plans for the evening and was sure that Jacques would be less than pleased when he discovered that the plans had been cancelled, but it was the right thing to do. Back in the main room of the first floor as Ezra handed Toby and Zeeney weapons, his wife Elizabeth, Ezra's wife of over thirty years, entered the room. She was still quite beautiful and Ezra loved her very much

"What is this? Are the three of you starting another adventure? You do recall how much trouble the last one caused. Why if it weren't for that adventure, Ezra and I might not be married today. When Father Pooles punished you, you had nothing better to do then pay attention to me. You even stopped lying to me, or did you?"

But Elizabeth's lighthearted manner stopped almost immediately as she became aware of the somber mood of the three best friends. Her new feeling was reinforced when General Lafayette descended the wide staircase and entered the room wearing his filthy uniform.

"What's wrong?" asked Elizabeth.

"Oh, maybe nothing, just a precaution. Toby and Zeeney saw something from their back porch that concerned them."

"What was it?" asked Elizabeth.

"Well, they saw many men in canoes headed toward the southern beach."

"What kind of men? Indians? The British?"

"We don't know for sure, but decided to treat it as a legitimate threat. I'm sure its nothing, but we can't take that chance."

With that the General excused himself and headed down the large center hall of the house toward the back entrance where his seven hundred and fifty troops had already assembled.

Chapter 51

Ezra, Toby, and Zeeney assembled on the front porch of the plantation house; soon Cyrus, Ezra's son, joined them. He had been brought up to date by his mother and already had his musket. Now there were four on the front porch, three older men and a boy who was not quite a man.

"What's the plan father?" Cyrus asked.

Ezra replied, "We wait here until General Lafayette brings his troops around and then we all head to the southern beach. We'll find out who these intruders are, if there are any, and what their intentions are."

Buckhorn and his band of braves arrived at the edge of the peach orchard and used the trees for cover. The full moon was still behind the trees on the far eastern shore of the bay and did not give much illumination. Buckhorn could see in the distance, across the opened field, what appeared to be three older men and a boy and they were carrying muskets. The torches that illuminated the porch made it very easy for Buckhorn to see the group but he also knew that because the porch was lighted and the field was dark, these old men could not see the movement of his braves.

"They did see us. Well, no matter, what can three old men and a boy do against my braves? I'll just have the braves with bows spread to the far perimeter of the peach orchard and order them to launch their arrows."

He gave the order to attack!

As Buckhorn watched the events unfold, he wondered, if the white men know we are here, are they just waiting to die? They are just standing on the porch. They must know what easy targets they are. If I were in their place, I'd take a more defensive stance. He watched the main body of his braves rush past him. This was to be the signal for his bowmen to aim their arrows and take down the four white men on the porch. They were in position and were about to release their arrows when movement on both sides of the house distracted them. Coincidentally, the brightness of the full moon illuminated the entire field just as Buckhorn ordered the attack. As soon as Ezra, Toby, Zeeney, and Cyrus saw the Indian braves rush from the peach orchard, they dropped to their knees. Luckily for all of them, their timing was perfect. They heard the arrows strike the wall behind them simultaneously. Even though they were under attack they could not help but look at the wall where they saw four perfectly aimed arrows that would have struck each of them in the upper chest. They turned back toward their attackers and immediately dropped to the floor. Again they heard thunk, thunk, as the second volley struck the wall .

"We can't go any lower," yelled Toby.

They did not have to.

To the left and right of the plantation house came close to a thousand Continental soldiers in full attack, with muskets aimed at Buckhorn's braves.

Buckhorn immediately ordered, "Fall back! Fall back!"

The order was unnecessary. As soon as the troops emerged from either side of the plantation house, Buckhorn 's braves knew what to do, run as fast as possible back to their canoes and get off the island. To attack this force would be suicide. The shots began to fire; the volleys were increasing in intensity. The braves dodged back and forth thinking that this would keep the shots from reaching them. Some of the unlucky ones were wrong; three fell, then four, then five. As soon as what was left of Buckhorn's raiding party hit the beach, they pushed the canoes into the water in stride. They also grabbed the paddles and started to stroke all in one motion, pulling them quickly from the shore. The soldiers volleys continued until they reached the beach and realized that the Indians were quickly moving out of range. The volleys slowly stopped. Ezra, Toby, Zeeney, and Cyrus arrived soon after. The old men were exhausted and collapsed on the beach. The soldiers, realizing that the Indians were well out of range, slowly turned and headed back to their campsite. Ezra, Toby and Zeeney finally recovered

As they sat on the beach, Toby said, "Ezra, Zeeney, do you know where we are? This is exactly where 'Deception' sank and we camped the first night on this island."

Zeeney looked around and said, "I think you're right. This is the exact spot, did you ever tell Cyrus the story?"

Ezra looked at Toby and Zeeney, smiled, and said to Cyrus, "Son, come sit by me. I want to tell you a story!"

The End

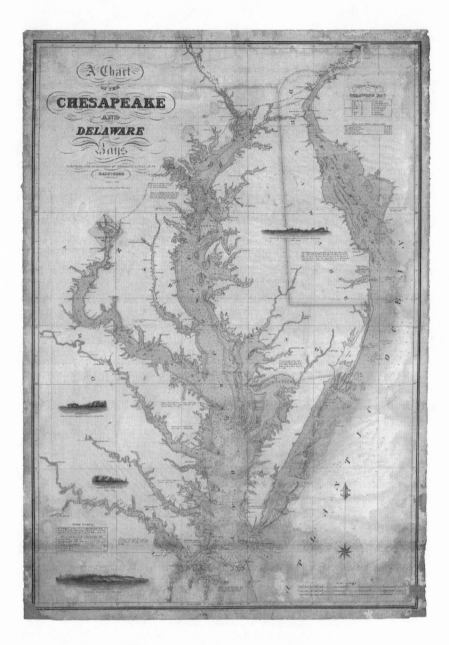

Chart courtesy of David Ramsey Map Collection.

Author's Note

This is a fictional story, Pooles Island is real, as are the other two unnamed islands, later they would become known as Hart and Miller Islands. North Point is also real and would become the site of the battle of North Point during the War of 1812. Pooles Island is located in the northwest portion of the upper Chesapeake, sitting at the mouth of the Gunpowder and Bush rivers. The adventurous Captain John Smith actually named the island Powell's Island, after one of his own crew-members, but over time the name has evolved to Pooles Island, most likely due to the spring fed water pools found on the island. The Baltimore Sun lauded the isle at the turn of the century; noting, "numerous wells of clear sparkling water are scattered about the island." The paper further commented that the water's pH was uniquely soft for the area, which was likely a factor in the prolific growth of crops and fruits.

The 280-acre, narrow island was purchased in 1808 by Peregrine Wethered, who ran it as a slave plantation. Whetered grew a lucrative wheat crop and was very prosperous, so much so that his produce was hailed with "the wonder and admiration of the farmers all along the bay." While the tract of land was plundered by British soldiers during the War of 1812, it quickly returned to profitability. The soil quality was exceptional to say the least, and much like the water the dirt was said to be quite distinctive from soil found in nearby counties. Early pioneers in the region noted that while chestnuts and pine trees were found in large numbers on the mainland, these plants were completely absent from Pooles Island.

The isle proved so desirable that in 1872, it was bought from Wethered's son by George Merrett, who planted 2,700 peach trees. Ten years later a farmer from Ohio purchased it from Merrett, remarking that he "had found a piece of Iowa soil in Maryland." This farmer added more peach orchards, and christened one of his varieties 'Pool's Island Best." It was marveled that the trees on the island grew to a size practically unheard of in other orchards. A late 19th century article reminded readers "that the abundant crops are produced…without the aid of fertilizers…"

The fruitful isle was first marked for a lighthouse in 1824, when Congress appropriated $5,000 for a beacon on six acres of land. John Donahoo was contracted to do the work on what would be the first of twelve lighthouses he would build on the Chesapeake Bay. A conical tower standing 40', six inches, the lighthouse is built from rough-hewn chunks of Port Deposit granite mortared together irregularly. The floor and foundation of the tower is made if cement, beneath which wooden pilings lends structural stability. The tower's diameter is 18' at its base, narrowing to nine feet at the top. Inside the structure, a spiral staircase made of spiral cut granite blocks ascends to the landing. The cast-iron lantern, which comprises 12-1/2 feet of the towers height, is cantilevered a few inches out from the mortared blocks. Stucco and whitewash were applied to the interior and exterior of the structure.

Improvements to the property commenced almost immediately. In 1828 Congress earmarked an additional $2,800 to build a fog bell tower. In 1857, at the behest of the newly established Lighthouse Board, a fourth-order Fresnel lens took the place of the old reflecting apparatus. In 1882, the keeper's dwelling was upgraded by an addition of an extra story, which made for three more rooms. The board reported that "…a new tin roof was then put on; the fencing was repaired and the lantern and fog bell tower were painted." Five years later a new front porch was added to the house, and a cow stable and poultry house were also built. In 1890, extra picket, post, and raining fencing was put up, and this combined with the plank and brick walkways to make the pastoral setting extremely pleasant for the keeper. A boathouse was added in 1892, along with a windlass to haul up watercraft.

Pooles Island was once the scene of an illegal but exciting prizefight that occurred in 1849. Maryland's governor decreed that no steamboat captain could transport spectators to the event and even called up troops to make certain that his orders were heeded. Nevertheless, pugilism fans found their way to the island on oystermen's skipjacks. The governor's troops were unable to shut down the festivities as their boat ran aground, and reportedly the spectators waved to the soldiers as they sailed back after the fight

In 1917, the year the United States entered World War I; the light station was placed under the jurisdiction of the US Army, who converted it into part of the Aberdeen Proving Ground. At this time the keeper was removed and the light was automated. The beacon was deactivated entirely in 1939, when the property was transferred to the War Department. The lens was removed from the lantern, and the keeper's house was torn down. A modern light now marks the channel east of Pooles Island.

The Pooles Island Lighthouse is currently inaccessible to the public, due both to its status as a military reservation and live artillery shells littering the grounds from Army training exercises. The Island's shore is also wearing away, and will probably require a quantity of riprap stone or bulkheads to arrest the erosion process. A nearby Army observation post, in fact, is almost in the water already.

Abandoned for nearly 50 years, the lighthouse was in poor condition before a massive Army and Coast Guard restoration effort. Nearly all of the stucco and paint had peeled off the tower's exterior, which seemed to be crumbling in places. In addition, the lantern, gallery, roof and balustrade were all badly in need of a paint job. The pedestal, which once sat beneath the lens had been removed and simply dumped on the ground with weeds and sand. While the lighthouse was in decent condition structurally, mortar joint cracks and fault lines needed to be repaired before they imperiled the tower's integrity.

In 1944 the Army submitted a proposal to make the lighthouse a National Historical Monument. As part of the process, the structure had to be thoroughly cleaned and structurally stabilized in a historically accurate manner. As the island has lacked a pier access since the late 19th century, an all terrain forklift had to be brought upon a barge equipped with a landing ramp. This forklift carried in a 1200-gallon water tank (to pressure wash the exterior) and other equipment and supplies to complete the project.

First the cast-iron lantern was brushed with wire, primed and painted with a high gloss, acrylic black hue. The primer used was designed specifically to stick to corroded metal urfaces. The prevalence of rust was due to organic residue from ivy growing along the sides of the tower, as well as algae and mildew build-up. This also caused a dark stain to appear around the middle of the tower, which was pressure washed with phosphate free detergent. Next, the three original window openings, long since bricked in, were opened up and scraped. Then freshly mixed mortar, rendered via cement mixer, was applied. This particular mortar was unique, as it had to be workable and strong, but also possess enough flexibility and tensile strength to compensate for the expansion and contraction of the granite under changing weather conditions. After the cement was applied, the Carpentry Shop of the

Directorate of Public Works fashioned three six-over-six double hung sashes to go along with the new pine windows. These were painted white, the same as in a 1910 photograph of the lighthouse.

After the mortar work had dried for two months, the entire structure was painted. Local Aberdeen resident Tim Hamilton generously volunteered his time for this undertaking, which was completed in a few days. Lambs wool rollers were used to apply the coats; using paint sprayer was unrealistic because of high winds on the island.

There are future plans to replace the tongue and groove mahogany door at the lighthouse, which is identical to Concord Point Light's door and is likely an original. A faint outline of the iron key box is still visible on the door's surface, and its cast-iron hinges are still present. There is also a great need to perform mortar and other repairs on the interior of the tower, which is in far worse shape that the outside. The lighthouse's keepers were mostly occupied with making needed repairs to the outside of the structure, so that the interior's mortar is very soft and easily crumbled. Once all the maintenance is completed, the Army plans to re-install the light on Pooles Island as a private aid to navigation. A plastic Fresnel lens and accompanying solar panel have already been set aside for this purpose.

Pooles Island has benefitted ecologically from the Army's stewardship. While habitat losses in the Chesapeake continue to mount, the reservation has proven to be a beautiful wildlife sanctuary. Man is no longer able to take advantage of the island's fertile soil, but eagles, blue herons, geese, osprey, and a small herd of deer are now thriving on their island home.

References

"Poole's Island Lighthouse Stabilization Project," Kaltenbacher, Aberdeen Proving Ground, Cultural Resource Office. Bay Beacon, Turbeyville, 1995.

Charts on cover and page 244 courtesy of Cartography Associates, David Rumsey Map Collection, www.davidrumsey.com

Location:
Located on Pooles Island near the entrance of the Bush and Gunpowder Rivers. Latitude: 39.2792 N Longitude: -76.2699 W.

Epilogue, except introduction, courtesy "Lightfriends.com"

Glossary

- Aft – At near or toward the stern
- Amidships – In the middle of the boat
- Bitter End – The final inboard end of a line
- Block - A pulley used to gain mechanical advantage
- Boom – A horizontal spar attached to the bottom edge of a sail riding on the mast and controlled by a sheet
- Bow – The front or forward part of a boat
- Bowsprit – A short spar extending forward from the bow. normally used to anchor the forestay
- Cleat – device used to hold a sheet or halyard
- Clew- Lower aft corner of the fore and aft sail
- Daggerboard – A board dropped vertically through the hull to prevent leeway movement. Maybe completely removed for beaching or downwind sailing
- Davits – Small cranes used to raise or lower small boats and light items from deck to water level
- Halyard – Lines used to haul up sails
- Head – Top corner of fore and aft sail
- Jib – A triangular foresail in front of the foremast
- Jibe – To go from one tack to another when running with the wind coming over the stern
- Keel – A fixed underwater part of a sailing boat to prevent sideways drift and to provide stability

- Larboard- Left side of boat when facing forward, now termed "port"
- Lee – The side sheltered from the wind
- Luff Up – To steer the boat into the wind thereby causing the sails to flap or luff
- Mainsheet – The line that hold a boom therefore controlling the sail
- Mast – A large wooden pole used to hold up a sail
- Nanticoke – Indigenous Native Americans that lived on the Chesapeake
- Ogooue River – A river in Africa, in the country of Gabon
- Outhaul – A line that adjusts tension along the foot of a sail along the boom
- Outriggers – Device used on small boats that bridge the beam of the boat and stabilize it through floatation on either side of the boat
- Pemmican – A dried, concentrated food consisting of pulverized meat, usually beef or buffalo, dried berries, and rendered fat. It can be stored for a long period of time. Modern day version, Beef Jerkey.
- Rigging – The lines that hold up the mast and move sails
- Rudder – A fin or blade attached to the hull stern for steering
- Sheet – A line that controls a sail
- Shrouds – A line running from the top of the mast and attached to the sides of the boat
- Starboard – The right side of the boat when facing forward
- Stay – A line from the top of the mast to the bow or stern of a boat
- Stern – After end of the boat
- Tack – The lower forward corner of a sail, also a term for moving the bow of the boat through the wind to change direction, from starboard to port,for example.

- Tiller - A bar or handle which fits to the rudder used for turning the boat

Courtesy – schoonerman.com – sailinglinks.com

About the Author

H. C. Creech lives with his wife Kerry and pets in Perry Hall, Maryland, a short distance from the Chesapeake Bay. He has spent his adult life in Graphic Arts and presently Color Management. He wrote this, his first novel, based on his passion for sailing, love of the Chesapeake, and fascination with Pooles Island.

A Note About the Type

This book was set in Garamond. The fonts are based on the fonts first cut by Claude Garamond (c.1480-1561). Garamond was a pupil of Geoffroy Tory and is believed to have followed the Venetian models, although he introduced a number of important differences, and it is to him that we owe the letter we now know as "old style." He gave to his letters a certain elegance and feeling of movement that won their creator an immediate reputation and the patronage of Francis I of France.

Designed by Mill Creek Press

Cover by Tom Scheuerman
Cover Chart courtesy of David Ramsey Map Collection

Printed and bound by BookSurge Publishing,
Charleston, South Carolina

2165250

Made in the USA